I forgot to Tell You

I forgot to Tell You

BALLET SCHOOL CONFIDENTIAL

CHARIS MARSH

DUNDURN

TORONTO

Editor: Shannon Whibbs
Design: Courtney Horner
Printer: Webcom

Library and Archives Canada Cataloguing in Publication

Marsh, Charis
     I forgot to tell you / Charis Marsh.
(Ballet school confidential)

Issued also in electronic formats.
ISBN 978-1-4597-0430-5

     I. Title. II. Series: Marsh, Charis. Ballet school confidential.

PS8626.A7665I46 2012   jC813'.6   C2012-903212-3

1 2 3 4 5   17 16 15 14 13

| Conseil des Arts du Canada | Canada Council for the Arts | Canada | ONTARIO ARTS COUNCIL CONSEIL DES ARTS DE L'ONTARIO |

We acknowledge the support of the **Canada Council for the Arts** and the **Ontario Arts Council** for our publishing program. We also acknowledge the financial support of the **Government of Canada** through the **Canada Book Fund** and **Livres Canada Books**, and the **Government of Ontario** through the **Ontario Book Publishing Tax Credit** and the **Ontario Media Development Corporation**.

Care has been taken to trace the ownership of copyright material used in this book. The author and the publisher welcome any information enabling them to rectify any refer-ences or credits in subsequent editions.

J. Kirk Howard, President

Printed and bound in Canada.

Visit us at
Dundurn.com
Definingcanada.ca
@dundurnpress
Facebook.com/dundurnpress

Dundurn	Gazelle Book Services Limited	Dundurn
3 Church Street, Suite 500	White Cross Mills	2250 Military Road
Toronto, Ontario, Canada	High Town, Lancaster, England	Tonawanda, NY
M5E 1M2	LA1 4XS	U.S.A. 14150

This book is for ...

My family, who read over my shoulder
while I was writing (it's very flattering!)
Adrian, who poked me whenever I
stopped making typing noises
Shannon, who made editing fun
Dundurn, because they were kind
enough to want to hear more about
Julian, Taylor, Kaitlyn, and Alexandra
You, because you were awesome enough
to pick up this book!

Chapter One

Alexandra Dunstan
Listening to Said the Whale, sewing pointe shoes, and done all my hmw. Life is good :)

There was a cool breeze blowing over English Bay. Alexandra stood at edge of the water, breathing in as she faced the wind. *Breathe. Breathe. Breathe.* She could feel her heart rate slowing down as the wind whipped around her face, cooling down her hot face. There. It was going to be all right, she was not going to let Grace win this time. She turned around and walked back toward the park behind the docks. She could already see Tristan and Julian there on the grass, and Grace; they were attracting a crowd around them. Apparently it was unusual to see people wearing ballet costumes in a park.

"Lexi, hurry up!" Grace called. "I'm cold! What are you doing?!" Alexandra sped up a bit, and as soon as she reached them began to unzip her hoodie and pull off her loose knitted pants, revealing her costume underneath.

"Sorry, just wanted to look at something on the water."

"Geez, can't you do that — I dunno, when I'm wearing clothes? I'm freezing here!"

"I'm sorry!"

Tristan silently reached out for her hand, and Alexandra stepped toward him on *pointe*, her foot on the makeshift wood sheet that had been placed on the grass for the occasion. She stepped into *arabesque*, and slowly bent into a *penche* as he reached for her other hand.

"Good, good!" the photographer said, bouncing in his excitement. "This is really neat! Lots of interest here. You're really bendy, aren't you?"

Beside Alexandra and Tristan, Julian reached out for Grace's hand, but Grace didn't want to pose with him. She shoved his hands away.

"Alexandra!" she hissed.

Alexandra ignored her. "Let's do a lift next," she suggested to Tristan. He nodded.

"Alexandra!" Grace said louder, loud enough that the photographer could hear.

"Is there a problem?" the photographer asked, putting his camera down for a second.

"Not really," said Grace. "It's just Alexandra has forgotten that Tristan and I were supposed to be paired together, and *she* was supposed to go with *Julian*, since Tristan and I are the first cast."

"Oh." The photographer scratched his head. "Uh, does it really matter? Because I'm really liking the photos I'm getting of these two." He looked at Alexandra and Tristan. "Hey, do you guys think it'd work if you could do something next to that tree over there? You boys grab that wood, and I'll start setting up the light. I think we could get something really mystical, really special, over here."

"Sure." Julian shrugged and started to help Tristan pick up the wood. Grace reached out and grabbed Alexandra's arm, gripping it so tight that it hurt. "Ow!" Alexandra said involuntarily. "Grace, let go of me."

Grace glared at her. "I think that *me* and Tristan should do the tree pose," she said loudly. "Since we are the first cast. And you and Julian are really only understudies."

Alexandra ignored her and followed the boys. They set the wood floor down on the grass, and the photographer carried on behind them, setting everything up around the tree and muttering to himself. Grace stepped onto the floor on the other side of Tristan and crossed her arms. "Tristan," she said sweetly: "I think we should do a lift. Want to do a fish?"

"No," said Tristan. "Not really. I don't want my face to be all red in the photo."

"Tristan!" Alexandra said suddenly, sounding excited. "Let's do that lift we were working on in *pas de deux* class yesterday, you know, the one where I'm in a backbend and you're holding me up? And then I can *port de bras* with my arms matching the trees, and it would look so sweet with the tree."

The photographer's face lit up. "That sounds exciting. Show me?"

Tristan and Alexandra went into their lift while Grace pouted at the side of them and Julian stood awkwardly on the grass, watching them.

"Maybe we could have your hair down?" the photographer suggested. "That way you'd look a bit like those woodland fairy things, what's the name, Greek mythology ..."

"Dryads?" Alexandra suggested, smiling at him.

"Yes, those! I like you. Now, just take that elaborate hair watchimacallit out of your hair — I bet that took you a long time to do! Yes, now — don't bother brushing it, just a moment." He reached out and expertly separated the thick coil left over from Alexandra's bun into many little coiling strands and smoothed it off her face. "Perfect. I like how pale you are, it really works with the setting. Now, Tristan, if you could just do that thing you were doing before — yes, perfect, I love the expression on your face!" The photographer clicked around them as Tristan struggled to hold Alexandra in place. She could feel his wrist shaking slightly under her back as he held her. They dropped out of the lift far before the photographer had tired of taking shots of them, Alexandra bending forward to counteract the strain on her back and Tristan frantically shaking his wrist.

"My wrist's still sore from *pas de deux* class," he muttered to Alexandra.

"Aw, muffin," she answered flippantly, straightening up and cracking her back.

"Hate you."

"Love you."

"Aw, love you, too."

"Do you think you could go up and do that thing again?" the photographer asked. "I feel like we've got something really special here. I'm really liking this." He stepped away from the tree and looked out toward the ocean, trying to judge the light. "The light's going to start to go soon, so I'll try and hurry up."

Alexandra and Tristan nodded. "One, two, three," Tristan said quietly, and on the count, Alexandra jumped and Tristan lifted, and she was in the air again. Her dark brown hair flowed down her back, creating an archway over Tristan's head under the canopy of the willow tree.

"I think I have it," the photographer said, his voice hushed so as not to jinx it. He stared at the screen on his camera. "I think I've got exactly what I want here. Thanks, guys. You can put your clothes back on now." Tristan and Alexandra gratefully began to pull on their clothes. Alexandra began to shiver as she pulled on her sweatshirt, her cold body reacting with relief to its warmth. "You guys can go now," the photographer said, turning to Julian and Grace. "Sorry for having you come out for nothing."

Grace glared at him. He bent down and began putting his camera away, pretending that he couldn't see.

"Thanks," Alexandra said, smiling down at the photographer. "Want me to help you put the stuff away?"

"I got it," he said, looking up and smiling. "Thanks for making my job so easy. I love doing a shoot with dancers. You guys already know about positive and negative space, you create interesting shapes right away without me having to say anything. And don't get me started on that crazy stuff you can do with your body —" He let out a low whistle and turned back to his equipment.

"Thanks, that's so sweet of you to say!" Alexandra said. She walked over to Tristan and linked her arm through his. "Bye-bye, Jules, bye, Grace. See you at rehearsal tomorrow morning." They began to walk down the Seawall, a long stretch of winding pavement with park on one side and the ocean on the other.

"Brrr, so cold," Tristan said, shivering spastically to emphasize his point.

"Yeah." Alexandra was busy thinking. "Do you think Mr. Demidovski will be upset with me that I was in the photo instead of Grace? I mean, they haven't even decided yet if they are going to let me have a cast of Swanhilda."

Tristan shrugged. He had gotten the role of Franz, and that was as far as his concern extended. "I dunno. Guess you'll find out."

Alexandra stepped away from his arm and onto the thick cement barrier between the ocean and the path. *Step, arabesque, step, arabesque.* She reached out suddenly for Tristan's hand, grabbing it as she almost fell in the water. She hopped off the barrier.

"Tristan," she said, as they continued along the path, "when we're old and married, do you want to live in a house around here? Of course, we'll be absolutely loaded then, too, so everything will work out perfectly. We won't be here very often, because we'll always be away guesting for all the top companies, and I will work for the Royal Ballet and you can work for ABT, so we won't see much of each other, but —"

Tristan stopped in the path and shoved his hands in his pockets. To Alexandra's surprise he looked upset. "What's wrong?"

"I don't think it's funny when you talk like that."

Alexandra stared at him, even more confused and getting mad about her confusion. "What do you mean? Talk like what?"

"Like — all the us getting married jokes and stuff."

"Why? It's just a joke. Obviously."

"I know. It just makes me upset, okay?" He kept his hands in his pockets and they carried on walking down the path.

Alexandra searched for the right words, but she didn't know what she had done wrong, and the more she thought about it, the more it seemed like Tristan was to blame. "Tris, you're being a butt. What's wrong?"

"It's just, okay, we make a good ballet partnership, well, now, right? But it's just weird to talk about us getting married and stuff. I know it's a joke, and I don't know why it feels weird now, but it does. So can you just stop it?"

"Uh, fine. Whatever. You could have just told me that instead of getting all upset."

"I did just tell you that."

"Whatever."

They walked in silence for a while, Alexandra waging a war within herself between curiosity and the need to make Tristan feel bad for being rude. Curiosity won. "Tristan, what happened?"

Tristan had been waiting for that question, and his thoughts flew out in a series of violently emotional scraps. "I told Julian I like him."

"Good? Bad?"

"Bad."

"Okay, sad."

"No! He's stupid. I met this guy. On the Internet."

"On the Internet? Tristan, wtf?"

"No, like, I know him sort of from before. But we didn't really — like, I still liked Julian, right? But, I don't know, I started following his blog, and then he added me on Facebook and we've been talking a lot and stuff. He's so smart, Lexi. The stuff he says, it's just really helping me right now."

"Wait, do I know this guy?"

"No." Tristan spoke far too fast, and a deep red blush rose from under his skin.

"Tristan Patel, tell me who it is! Right now!"

"No! You don't know him."

"I totally do, you are a horrible liar! Come onnn, Tris, I won't tell anyone, I swear." Tristan shook his head, and Alexandra sulked. "You suck."

They began to walk across the green grass of the park, cutting a wide swath around a group of young adults playing frisbee. Alexandra felt self-conscious in her knit pants, the skirt of her costume hanging over it, and her thick blue academy hoodie over top. The bus stop was empty, and Alexandra sat down on the bench, tucking her legs up and sitting cross-legged. Tristan sat down next to her and pulled out his Thermos of green tea, using it to warm his hands. "Your parents still bugging you about stuff?" he asked.

"Yeah," Alexandra said, grimacing. She'd gone to her family dentist and then he'd had a talk with her mom afterwards, saying that he had suspected that she was throwing up. *How was I supposed to know that dentists could tell that from your teeth?* She'd accidentally told Tristan that her parents were upset about something, and now he wouldn't let it go.

"So, what was it? What did the perfect Miss Alexandra Dunstan of the perfect homework and dedication to ballet do to piss her parents off?"

"Tristan! Stop it, okay?"

"No, seriously, tell me, I can't picture it. Wait, I know, you didn't do enough homework, that's it, right?"

"Tristan, I'm this close to slapping you."

The bus came, and they got on, making their way to the back. "You going home now?" Tristan asked, holding on to the bus bar, his slim body swaying back and forth with the movement of the vehicle.

"Yeah. I've got so much homework. I'm afraid that I'm going to be doing what Andrew did in his last year next year."

"Andrew Lui? San Francisco Ballet Andrew? Why, what'd he do?"

"You don't remember? When he was in grade twelve. He'd come for one day, hand all of his homework in and get the homework he'd missed, then he couldn't show up for the next day because he'd have to finish the homework he got from the day before, and he just repeated that all year."

Tristan shrugged. "He graduated, it's all good."

"Yeah, but I'd like to graduate with an average a little better than his."

"Why? Even if you do go to university or something it won't be for, like, a long time."

Alexandra shrugged. "I don't know. It's like a comfort thing for me. Homework, it's this constant, and if I'm getting good grades it's like even if dance or something isn't going well, at least I have good grades and I can be happy about that, you know?"

"Not really," Tristan said. "But okay." The bus stopped downtown and they transferred, heading over to the North Shore.

"Are we friends?" Tristan asked suddenly.

Alexandra frowned at him, confused. "What is wrong with you, Tristan? Of course we are."

"Just checking." Tristan shrugged. "I don't know, sometimes I feel like we are so close and we talk so much, but I don't actually know anything about you. That's what I like about … that guy. We talk, and it's like we're having this really open, real conversation."

Alexandra raised her eyebrows. "Uh-huh. Tristan, I'm kind of worried about you. I mean, if you're just talking to him on the Internet —"

"I know him from real life, though! It's not like that."

"Soooo," said Alexandra, starting to smirk, "what exactly happened with Julian? Did you find out if he's gay or not yet?"

"I don't know!" Tristan exploded.

"What do you mean you don't know?"

"Like, okay, so this was after men's class, and we were walking to the bus stop, right?"

"Yeah. Wait, when was this?"

"Like, two weeks ago."

"Wow, rebound much?"

"Shut up. Anyway, so we were walking, and I said, uh, I said —" Tristan stopped, suddenly awkward.

"Whaaat? C'mon, tell me. What? What? What?"

"Well, I was like, 'I don't know if you are gay, or straight, or whatever, but I like you, and I thought you should know that.'"

"And?"

"I don't know! He just ignored it and started talking really fast about something else. I know he heard me. I don't know. He's stupid."

"What the — yeah, that's super weird. Julian's strange."

"Yeah. Whatever. I'm over it."

The bus pulled up to Alexandra's stop, and she stood up. "Bye, love you, see you tomorrow. Don't talk to Internet freaks."

Alexandra stood at the window of the studio on the top floor of the academy. She could see into the apartment across from the studio, and she absentmindedly watched the people inside to take her mind off the pain from stretching. She was getting better; she could almost hook her chin over her toe when it was stretched out in front of her on the *barre* now.

Jessica came in, took one look at Alexandra in the empty room, and snorted. "Do you have any friends?"

Alexandra ignored her. She had her headphones in; they could have been louder. With excessive noise, Jessica set her bags down and began to stretch. Grace followed her in a few moments later, and they sat together, talking and stretching. Alexandra kept looking out the window, stretching her foot above her head. Ever since Grace had gotten first cast of Swanhilda in the June production of *Coppelia*, it had been like she had jumped a level and Alexandra had been left behind. Alexandra wondered to herself what she had ever liked in Grace. *What I don't get*, Alexandra thought, *is why the academy always casts her. She doesn't have a good body type; she doesn't do well at competitions. She just isn't very good.*

Alexandra could hear Grace and Delilah's conversation get louder, and she pressed her face into her shin, trying to ignore them. "The whole time, she was just sucking up to the photographer, and she didn't even tell him that she was just the understudy! It was unbelievable. Like, who does she think she is?"

Alexandra heard Jessica laugh. "Well, if she's that desperate, maybe she should have it. I don't know how you deal with her, she's so —"

Alexandra could feel them turn to look at her, and she automatically pulled her foot even closer to her head.

"Do you think she's listening to us? She totally is. So creepy!"

Alexandra had had about all she could stand. She untangled her limbs, picked up her bag, and walked out of the room, heading downstairs to the large airy main studio where they had class.

Downstairs the studio had almost filled up. "Tris, save me a spot?" she called from the doorway.

"Fine," Tristan complained. He set his water bottle on the patch of floor by the *barre* next to him.

Alexandra wandered off to the academy's office. She needed to talk to the office's person-in-charge-of-every-thing, Gabriel. She had thought about it the night before, and if she wasn't going to get a cast of Swanhilda she would have to work even harder this year and get out by September. She needed a new school, new teachers, new air to breathe, and people that believed in her. So she had made a list of things she needed to accomplish by then.

Grace's mom was waiting at the office, leaning on the counter with a serene smile on her face as she surveyed the studio lobby, watching everyone go in and out. "Oh, hi, Lexi, what do you need?"

Alexandra smiled at her. "Hi. Just needed to talk to Gabriel."

"Oh, what about?"

Alexandra looked away to the inner office, hoping that Gabriel wouldn't suddenly appear and she wouldn't have to state what she wanted with Grace's mom watching. "Just needed to get some bills from my privates."

"Oh, yes," said Grace's mom sympathetically. "Those bills, they're horrendous." She moved in closer to Alexandra so that she could whisper into her ear. "Do you know what I always tell Grace? It's because they're all foreigners. Foreigners treat money differently than we do. They don't realize what a privilege it is to teach our children."

Alexandra fought an instinctive urge to noticeably wince, and settled for moving away from her. "Oh?"

"Well, I have to go now; I can't spend any more time hanging around here ... always so busy! Good luck, sweetie." Grace's mother exited the office in a swirl of expensive clothing and red lipstick. If I'm ever like that I'm going to shoot myself, Alexandra thought.

Gabriel emerged from the office like an over-sized magic genie the second Grace's mother had left. "Alexandra," he said with relief.

Alexandra stared at him in surprise, caught off guard; he was usually far less happy to see her. She shook her head and rattled off the list of questions she had compiled since she had last seen him. "Gabriel, can I start having privates again with Mr. Demidovski for a competition in the summer? And can I book studio A for one slot a week starting on the sixteenth, because Mrs. Mallard is going to be coaching me for my Solo Seal? And can I have a bursary sheet to apply for a bursary?"

Gabriel nodded and dived under his desk to rummage in the cardboard boxes where he kept his most important papers, never fully trusting the ancient academy computer. "She just got divorced," he mumbled under the table.

"What? Who?" Alexandra rose to her *demi-pointe* and leaned over the counter so that her head was on the same side of the counter as Gabriel's. "Who's getting divorced, Gabriel?"

"Her. Grace's mother. April Kendall." Gabriel closed his mouth and pulled out a bursary form. He stood up. "Here you go."

"How do you know?" Alexandra took the form from Gabriel.

"She told me," he said uncomfortably.

"Weird ..."

Gabriel nodded his agreement.

"See ya, Gabriel. Thanks." Alexandra left the office, frowning with the news she had just gotten. Why would April tell Gabriel about that? How would that even come out? "Hey, person who I sign my daughter up for dance lessons with, I'm getting divorced?" Was she trying to hit on him? Ew!

Alexandra was walking back toward class when she saw her mother outside. She paused, surprised, and started walking toward the glass side doors to say hi and ask her what she was doing at the academy. As Alexandra drew closer, she saw that Grace's mother was talking to her mother, and they both looked angry. April Kendall's posture was drawn up and stiffened in the way she did when she was mad, and Beth was gesticulating, clearly getting over-emotional. She walked on the side of the hall where she was hidden by the wall but could still see out, and walked until she could hear their conversation. "Everybody knows that your daughter doesn't have a scrap of talent!" Alexandra could hear her Beth say. "I think it's just sickening how you think you can use money to buy your daughter what she should be working for. What are you teaching her? That mommy's going to buy her false rewards for the rest of her life?"

"You are completely out of line," Alexandra could hear April hiss. "You are crazy. My daughter is a better dancer than your daughter, and you just can't handle that."

"Uh-huh. Tell me, is Grace still going to get the same roles now that you and Tomas have split? Maybe you should have thought about that before —"

Alexandra never got to hear what came before, because she turned around, hearing a sound on the steps behind her. Taylor was sitting on the steps, her blue eyes wide in surprise. "Did you hear that?" she whispered to Alexandra.

"Yeah. What the frick?"

"I don't know. Your mom was walking this way, and then Grace's mom came out, and they were talking normally about something, and then all of a sudden they just started yelling. Like that. Is it true?"

Alexandra thought. "I don't know. It seems really bizarre, but — my mom wouldn't make that up. I can't believe she didn't tell me about it!"

"Maybe she didn't know before," Taylor suggested.

"I wonder if Grace knows," Alexandra said suddenly, the thought popping into her brain. An image of Grace filled her brain, so smug and self-righteous, with her thick golden-brown hair and brown eyes, never yelled at, even by Mr. Moretti, never hated by any of the teachers. Alexandra sat down next to Taylor and stared at the window. Beth was walking away from April, her steps long and firm as she crossed the street to her car.

"I guess she doesn't need to do anything here after all," Taylor said, giggling.

"Wouldn't that be the most horrible thing in the entire world?" Alexandra asked, still thinking about Grace. "Imagine thinking that you were really good at something your entire life and then finding out that no, actually someone had been just paying for everyone to pretend you were good?"

Taylor shrugged. "It wouldn't be that bad," she said. "Of course it would be better to be actually good, but …"

Alexandra stood up suddenly. "Don't tell Grace," she ordered Taylor. She suddenly felt strangely protective of Grace. Grace had been horrible to her all year, but there were some things that nobody should have to find out. Especially by being told by Taylor, Alexandra thought, struggling to not roll her eyes at Taylor's hair. Taylor had decided to do a bun on either side of her head today instead of just one bun, and in Alexandra's highly judgmental opinion, she looked like an idiot. "Let's go to class, we're going to be late."

As Alexandra stood at her spot next to Tristan at the *barre*, she had another thought, looking across the room at Grace warming up. What if she does know that her mom has been buying her roles? And she's just been lying to me all these years? Well, it's not like she could tell me if it's true, but still, what an annoying thing to do. The more that Alexandra thought about it, the less she believed that Grace didn't know, and the more furious she got. All those times that I lost roles to her and she acted like it was just because she was better than me!

Chapter Two

Julian Reese:
K'naan's the best ... he makes me want to rap, but
then I remember how stupid I sound when I try :p

Julian woke up feeling down. He got up out of bed, his
muscles sore from yesterday's class, and pulled on his
clothes. He was too tired to face showering today. He
shoved his books and binder in his backpack, barely
checking to see if they were the ones that he needed
that day. He pulled on his hoodie and jacket, pulling the
hood up. No one was in the kitchen, so he grabbed his
lunch and a persimmon and left, not bothering to get
himself any cereal.

Outside, the world was just as grey as he felt inside.
The rain was a steady downpour, dripping down every
building, but not violent enough to flood the streets.
Julian shifted his backpack onto his shoulders and
began walking to the bus stop, biting into his persimmon. With every bite he also got rainwater. He waited
for the bus, thinking about nothing. He'd been thinking
about nothing a lot lately. It wasn't that he had nothing
to think about: it was more that he had so much to think
about that the only way to handle it was to think about
none of it. So he stood in the rain and watched the sky's

dark blue slowly lighten to a grey as the sun came up behind the clouds. He didn't even bother turning on his iPod. The bus came and he got on, sitting on one of the benches at the front.

At McKinley, the halls were empty. He could hear his feet, loud in the usually noisy halls. The Super Achiever's program students were the only ones that had classes this early in the morning. He got to his chemistry class and sat down in a seat in the back. *Oh.* He remembered that he had homework for today. Basic stuff, just some balancing. Stuff that he should have been able to do in his sleep; only not literally, and he had gone to sleep instead of doing it last night. He reached in his backpack and searched through his binder for the sheet that he was supposed to have completed. His binder was a mess of all the subjects he was taking thrown together: chemistry and biology and socials and math and English. He finally found it, between a paper on the Canadian parliamentary system and a handout sheet on Macbeth. He looked up; Alexandra sat in front of him, but her seat was empty today. Tristan wasn't there yet, either. He turned to the side, looking for a possible candidate. There. Emily. "Hey." His voice was apologetic. He shoved his hoodie back off his head, showing his face. "Did you do the homework? I sorta fell asleep instead." He smiled.

Emily blushed. "Yeah. Want to copy mine? I think you have time, here ..." Emily passed the paper over to him.

"Thanks." Julian quickly began to copy her work.

"You dance, right?"

"Yup." Julian concentrated on his paper. While Emily watched Julian, and Julian concentrated on copying, neither of them noticed Mr. Kang coming up behind them.

"Is that the homework sheet? Cheating is a zero," Mr. Kang commented calmly. "That's a zero for you, Julian, and you, too, Emily." He walked back to the front.

"Damn it." Julian rubbed his forehead with both of his hands, trying to rub out everything that kept going wrong in his life lately. "I'm sorry, Emily."

"It's okay," Emily reassured him. "It's not worth much. I don't know why he's making such a big deal of it; everyone copies homework for his class."

"Yeah." Julian sunk his face down into his hands and spent the rest of the class in that posture, trying to sleep without looking like he was asleep.

Julian waited on the steps for Charlize to pick him up. He and Taylor had another private with Theresa today, even though they were done with competition. When she said that she wanted to continue coaching him every week, Julian had said no, because he didn't know where he would get the money.

"That's all right," Theresa had said, smiling. And then somehow, Julian wasn't sure how it had happened, she had found a couple that was willing to pay for her to coach Julian. "A scholarship," Theresa said. "They love to support young people." The couple had come to watch Julian rehearse a few times, but they had seemed more interested in watching Theresa coach than Julian dance, and Theresa had been a nervous mess each time they had come. Taylor couldn't understand why they were there; Theresa had told Julian not to tell Taylor about the scholarship. Julian told her that they were old fans of Theresa's, which he suspected was the truth.

Charlize took the corner into McKinley's school parking lot a little too hard and narrowly missed hitting a grade twelve student's BMW. Julian walked over and climbed in. He had barely closed the door before Charlize had turned the car in a large circle and sped away again. She drove through the old trees that lined the streets of the rich residential neighbourhood surrounding McKinley. "How are you?" she asked Julian, looking at him in her mirror.

"Good," Julian said. He looked at Taylor, who was sitting in the front seat. *Still mad?* he mouthed. She nodded.

Charlize pressed hard on her horn, startling a nanny crossing the road with two little children. Julian winced as one of the kids started to cry, burying her small blond head in her nanny's shoulder. "What's wrong, Charlize?" he asked.

"Oh, I'm fine," Charlize said. "Just a little tired. Agh! I wish they'd just stop handing out licences in Richmond, nobody in that stupid suburb can drive." She cut off a red car on her left and slipped in front of a black Hummer. Julian stared out the window and suppressed the urge to jump out and moon the Hummer. *There is absolutely no reason to own a Hummer. Period. You will be eaten first in the event of an alien invasion.*

Julian reached for his phone as it began to vibrate.
It was Taylor.

She cried.

When?

This morning.

They were on the bridge to downtown now. Charlize
grabbed the box of Tim Hortons doughnuts that sat
between her and Taylor and shoved it backwards to
Julian. "Quick, eat it," she said. "If you don't, I will. I just
can't control myself when it comes to doughnuts."

Julian shrugged and opened the box. *Yay!* There
was one of the maple-covered doughnuts with a hole in
the centre. Those were Julian's favourite, he loved the
maple, but he hated the yucky cream filling that was
in the centre of the kind without holes. "Charlize," he
asked, swallowing a bite of the doughnut. "Where did
you go to school?"

In front of him, Charlize tensed. "What an odd
question," she said, laughing.

"I was just wondering," Julian said innocently. "Since
you are so upset about Taylor dropping out."

"That is irrelevant. Nobody wants their kids to make
the same mistakes they did. I graduated from high
school, and I went to college."

"Oh."

"I went to at least ten different high schools," Charlize
suddenly admitted. "I didn't like school, and if you don't
attend, they kick you out."

Taylor turned to her mother, surprised. "You never told me that."

"Why would I?"

They drove in silence as Taylor sewed her *pointe* shoes and Julian tried to eat his doughnut as slowly as possible. *Mmmm ... sugar ...*

The studio was full when they got there. All the Youth Company dancers were rehearsing in the downstairs studios. They had a run of shows coming up in the Interior, so they had been rehearsing constantly. Taylor and Julian headed up to the top floor, where the smaller studios were located. The door to the studio, usually open, was closed this time. Julian put his ear against it, listening. "I don't hear anything," he reported back to Taylor. He slowly turned the old glass knob and pushed open the door.

The sunlight coming through the windows made the dust in the air appear to dance. "I wonder when the last time they cleaned up here was," Taylor said. Her voice seemed loud in the emptiness of the room.

Julian shrugged. He put his bag down and began to put his soft shoes on as Taylor taped her toes. "Ah, hello," a voice said from behind them. Taylor screamed.

Behind them, Mrs. Demidovski stepped back, startled by the noise. "What you scream? No scream," she said. Her accent was thick due to her surprise.

"Uh — where did you come from?" Julian asked.

Mrs. Demidovski laughed. "Come here," she said, motioning them over. She walked toward a purple door at the back of the room. Julian had always assumed that it led into a closet for costume storage. Mrs. Demidovski took a key out of her pocket and opened it up. Julian and Taylor hung back. "Come on," Mrs. Demidovski said impatiently. "What, you afraid of Mrs. Demidovski?"

Julian shook his head, and he and Taylor followed Mrs. Demidovski into a small room. It was so small that it could have been a closet at some point. "This building, used to be bank," Mrs. Demidovski explained. "Here, here was a —" she paused, searching for the words. "Keep safe, money, paper."

"A safe?" Julian asked.

"Yes, yes, keep safe. Never mind, now it is Mrs. Demidovski's office. Come, sit down." Mrs. Demidovski shut the door behind them, and they walked over to the desk.

"How are you?" she asked, as always. She sat down in the only chair as Julian and Taylor stood awkwardly. "Sit! Sit, uh?"

Julian and Taylor sat on the ground. The floor was covered with a thick blue carpet, completely different from the rest of the academy. It was so comfortable that Julian felt like lying down on it and having a nap. "How are the privates with Theresa?" Mrs. Demidovski asked. "She teach you a lot?"

"Yes." Julian nodded. "She's awesome."

"I come and watch." Mrs. Demidovski did not say it as a question. She turned to Taylor. "And you? How is for you? Do you learn? Are you working hard?"

Taylor shrugged. "Good, I think."

"You just think? No good. Must know." Mrs. Demidovski sighed. "Julie, go get Mrs. Demidovski water."

Julian nodded and left the room in search of the water cooler. He hoped that Theresa wouldn't come and only see an empty studio. He hurried back with the small paper cone of water.

He pushed open the door quickly. "Here you go, Mrs. —" he stopped. Taylor was sitting in Mrs. Demidovski's chair crying while the older woman fussed over her.

"What's wrong?" Julian asked, awkwardly holding the cone of water.

"Nothing," Mrs. Demidovski snapped. "Give me the water. Thank you." She took the cone from him and slowly swallowed the whole thing, her wrinkly neck moving as she did so. She passed the cone back to Julian and turned back to Taylor, patting her awkwardly on the head. "You very pretty girl," she said awkwardly. Mrs. Demidovski was clearly not used to giving compliments. "You very beautiful, very happy, don't worry. Work hard, you become a good dancer. You have a very clean, strong body."

Taylor nodded, sniffing.

Julian stood there, confused. He wasn't sure what to do. Was he supposed to leave? To agree with Demidovski? It was all so painfully awkward, he hated it when people cried. He heard a loud thump in the studio. "I think Theresa's here," he said.

Taylor blew her nose.

"Quickly, quickly," Mrs. Demidovski hurried her. "Go practice."

Taylor hopped off the chair, and Julian was relieved to see she wasn't crying anymore. She followed Julian out of the room into the studio.

It was Theresa. Julian smiled, glad to see her. "Hello Jules," she said, smiling back at him. She was dressed in her old ballet clothes like usual. She was the only ballet teacher Julian had who did. All his other teachers wore something they could move in, but it was still street clothing. Theresa wore her tights and soft shoes and bodysuit and did her hair up to teach them. Julian found it a bit odd, but endearing at the same time. He tried not to look at the bones on her chest. She always wore pale bodysuits, and Julian could see all of her bones through the light fabric, and it made him want to wince, like the videos about starving people in Social Studies class. The worst was her boobs: he could see her nipples and then a flat oval patch on each side where a boob should have been but wasn't.

"How are you two?" Theresa asked. "Warm?"

They shook their heads. "We were talking to Mrs. Demidovski," Julian defended himself.

"That's okay. You wouldn't want to leave Mrs. Demidovski. All right then, I'll give you a few minutes to warm up." She walked over to the CD player and began fiddling with it. Julian swung his chest down to his legs, hanging there to stretch out his hamstrings. He was still so sore from men's class yesterday. He walked slowly backwards, still hanging down.

"Taylor," he hissed. She was on the floor tying the ribbons on her *pointe* shoes. "What was wrong?"

"Nothing," she whispered back. "Tell you later."

"Why not now?"

"Later!"

"A little bit warmer?" Theresa asked, pulling on a pink knit ballet shrug.

"Yeah." Julian nodded.

"Now, Julian," Theresa said, looking at him. "I want to teach you something a little bit different today." She walked over to him and turned around, so that they were both facing the mirror. She placed his hands on her hips, and adjusted so that she was on *demi-pointe* and her left leg was in *arabesque,* facing the side wall. "Now, lift."

Julian *plied* on his right leg and bent his arms at the same time, and when he came up again he had pressed her above his head. "Good!" Theresa said excitedly. "Very good! Now lower me down, gently, gently, on my leg so I can balance, make sure you aren't tilting my hips so that I will fall. Very good! Much better Julian, you improve so fast."

Out of the corner of his eye, Julian saw Taylor roll her eyes.

After their private and regular classes, Julian walked out of the studio with Taylor. "So why were you crying?" he asked.

"I told you, it was nothing." Taylor walked slowly, and Julian struggled to keep pace with her, but it was worth it if she would just tell him what was up.

"Come on, you have to tell me."

"It was just, she was talking about how I needed to get better, and how I needed to work on my *pirouettes*, and how I wasn't ready for competition and exams, and what was I planning to do next summer because she thinks that I should stay at the academy and study, and then I just started crying because I'm not good enough." She burst into tears again as Julian watched, horrified. He had not been expecting that again.

"Taylor, you're good!"

"Not *really* good, not like Lexi," Taylor answered, blowing her nose in the napkin Julian handed her.

"Well — maybe you just need to work harder," Julian suggested.

Taylor instantly stopped crying and froze, staring at Julian. "What?"

Julian felt unsure about where this conversation was heading. "Well, if you want to be better, you probably just need to work harder."

Taylor pressed her lips together and stomped her foot.

"Did you just stomp your foot? Seriously?" Julian stared at her, astonished. "I thought girls only did that in movies."

"*I* need to work?" Taylor exclaimed disbelievingly.

"Well, not you, specifically, I mean everyone does —"

"I can't believe that you, of all people, said that."

"Hey! What do you mean me of all people? What's that supposed to mean?"

"You know."

"No, I don't." Julian stared at her. Their sides had switched suddenly; he could feel anger welling up inside of him. Julian was nice until he snapped, and then words seemed to pour out of his mouth. Taylor looked sorry that she had brought anything up.

"Well, you never work as hard as everyone else," Taylor explained. Her voice sounded as calm and convinced as if she was explaining that it rained a lot in Vancouver, or that her hair was blond.

"That's not true!"

"Yes, it is. All the teachers think so."

"Theresa doesn't."

"Yeah, because she's super weird and, like, obsessed with you!"

Between them there was a sudden, shocked silence. Julian could see from Taylor's face that she had not meant to say it, and his temper went down, replaced by confusion.

"What do you mean?"

"Well, don't you think it's a bit weird? That *she's* a bit weird? She only wants to coach you."

"She coaches you, too."

"So you can practise *pas de deux* because she knows it would look weird if she practised with you."

"That's not true."

"Whatever."

Taylor began to walk toward the bus stop. Julian ran after her. "She's not weird," he said, catching up. "She just wants to coach the dancers she actually likes."

Taylor shrugged. "Okay."

"What do you mean okay?"

"Crap, my bus." Taylor ran for her bus, leaving Julian behind. He was very confused. He turned around and started walking toward his bus. It started to rain, a light drizzle through the sun. He pulled on his sweatshirt. *I do work. She's wrong. She's the one that dropped out of school, anyway, so she has no right to say anything.* He knew Taylor was right about Theresa being weird, but she was a ballet dancer. It wasn't like she was going to be normal. *Besides,* Julian thought, *why shouldn't she just coach me if that's what she wants? Maybe she just thinks I'm the best dancer. That's probably it! I bet Taylor's just jealous.* The more Julian thought about his theory, the more convinced he was that he was right. He ran and got on the SkyTrain, heading out to Burnaby. He wanted to go to Metrotown mall to find a present for his brother River. It was River's birthday in a few days, he was going to be five, and Julian wanted to get him something.

The SkyTrain was crowded, and Julian had to make room where there wasn't any, taking his bag off and shoving it onto the ground. He couldn't reach the rail, so he held on to the train ceiling with his fingers. Around him was a cacophony of people, speaking different languages, listening to different music that was coming out of leaky headphones, smelling of sweat and cheap perfume and different foods. Julian suddenly felt overwhelmingly homesick. He didn't want to be *home*, exactly, but he wanted to feel like he did at home, where everybody basically thought the same things and smelled the same, and ate the same food. He wanted to be able to speak an opinion and have everyone nod in agreement, not look at him like he was an alien. He was sick of people telling him that he didn't work hard enough, and he was sick of the other students gossiping about him, and he missed his old best friend, Caspian, and how they could talk about things for hours without having weird silences. He wanted someone to hug him.

He got off the train at Metrotown station, and walked across the overpass that connected the train to the mall, his head down as he passed the groups of wannabe gangs in their cheap imitation rap clothes. "Hey!" one of the boys shouted. Julian didn't turn around, walking faster until he had safely entered the doors. He wished he didn't still look so young; it would be nice to look more like the sixteen years he was, instead of having permanent baby-face. It was fine in dance, most people looked younger than their age there, but in the outside world it sort of sucked. He walked down, heading toward Toys "R" Us. He'd forgotten what Metrotown was like. It was just so depressing, the waves of people spending and worrying about money, the cheap items, the smell of plastic and fast food. It was the most horrible thing. Julian thought that that must be what Las Vegas was like, except a trillion times more so; the smell and feel of hundreds of people worrying about money. He missed that about the Island; there it hadn't mattered so much if you had money, or what you spent it on.

"Julian!" Julian turned around. There was Tristan, standing on the top of the escalator with Delilah, waving at him. "Julian!"

Julian hurried toward him, breaking through the crowds of people that were between him and Tristan. Tristan stepped off the escalator, and they stood looking at each other awkwardly for a second. "What are you doing here?" Tristan asked suddenly, at the same moment that Julian said, "I thought you weren't talking to me!"

They both laughed nervously. "Um —" Julian looked around. "I need to find a present for my baby brother. Something cheap and not terrible. And I'm not supposed to get him candy, Daisy got mad at me for that last time."

"Cool. I'll help if you want; I was just here to get a pair of jeans."

"The ones you were going to get last time, at Zara, were so sweet," Delilah interjected.

"I *wasn't* going to get those ones; they make my legs look weirdly shaped. The zippers made my calves look bowed." Tristan turned back to Julian. "Um, so are we good?"

"Uh — yeah." Julian shrugged. "I mean, why wouldn't we be?"

Tristan's smile dropped. "Uh, yeah. Okay then."

They began to walk toward the back of the mall. "Tristan," Julian said suddenly, "can I ask you a question?"

Tristan stood still. "Uh, yeah, sure, what? What is it?"

Julian kept walking, his head down as he thought of the right words. "Um, me and Taylor, we were sort of having this argument — and then she said something, and I'm not sure if it was true, and I don't think it was true, and maybe she didn't mean it. I was wondering if you could tell me what you thought."

"Did she tell you she liked you?"

"What? No! She was telling me that —"

"She does, you know. Like you."

Julian was confused. This is not the direction the conversation was supposed to be going in. "Maybe. Anyway, she told me that I didn't work hard, and —"

"You don't."

"— that Theresa coached me because she was weird. Wait, what?"

"You don't work hard, and Theresa's coaching you because she has issues." Tristan shrugged. "Fact. Do you like Taylor?"

"Of course he does, have you seen Taylor?" Delilah said impatiently. "Where are we going?"

Julian didn't know how to respond. How could Tristan be agreeing with Taylor? He opened his mouth to argue, but he didn't know what he wanted to say. He saw a Chapters to his left. "Oh!" He veered suddenly around and began to walk swiftly in the direction of the books, deliberately leaving them behind. Tristan and Delilah had to half-run to catch up.

"Can your brother even read yet?" Tristan asked.

"Yeah, of course," Julian said proudly. "He's a Reece. He's been reading since he was three."

"Okay then. Weird. Why do you even remember that?"

"I taught him," Julian explained. "It was cool, first I was teaching him to read *Goodnight Moon*, and then he started reading Dr. Seuss and Robert Munsch books and now —"

Tristan yawned, bored.

"Anyway, he likes books. Come on!" Julian sped up and the three of them hurried into Chapters, with Tristan and Delilah giggling at how excited Julian was about it. "Here," Julian said, guiding them to the children's section.

"It says eight to ten," Delilah said, peering around.

"He's a good reader," Julian said impatiently. He walked up and down the aisles, pulling books out until he had a large tower in his arms. Then he sat down on the floor, spreading his legs out to either side of him so that the books were sitting in front of him. He began to organize them into piles; "Too expensive. Too expensive, but love. Love. Not so good, but cheap."

Tristan had wandered off, and he came running back, excited. "Jules! I love this book."

"Show me?" Julian reached up and took it. On the cover was a picture of Theresa Bachman as Odette, the white swan. The cover said: *The Diary of a Ballerina: Theresa Bachman*.

"I've read it like a thousand times," Tristan said, sitting next to Julian and leaning on his leg so that he could reach the book and turn the page to the one he wanted to show him. "Or, at least four times."

The page Tristan had turned to had the section title: "Isaac's Departure." Julian began to read aloud, Tristan leaning over his shoulder on one side, and Delilah on the other. "Isaac's departure hit Theresa hard. Her performances in the weeks afterwards were lacklustre at best. It took artistic director and long-time friend

Merhdad Anton's intervention to help Theresa move on." Julian paused. "Who's Isaac?" he asked. He never knew any of the famous ballet dancers and choreographers that Tristan and the rest were always going on about, but feeling stupid about not knowing for the last year had made him immune to embarrassment. Now he just asked, and ignored it when they made fun of him. He'd learned a lot that way; Tristan was like a living dance Wikipedia.

"This dancer who was in Vancouver Ballet's corps. God, Julian, you really need to learn more about the dance world," Tristan explained, rolling his eyes. "But, see, look —" he turned the page, and Julian stopped, surprised.

"He looks so much like me!" he said, shocked. The boy in the black-and-white photo, who must have been twenty years old at least, looked remarkably similar to Julian. His jaw stuck out more, and his nose was bigger, and he had more muscles; but his hair looked like the same shade as Julian's, from what could be told from the grey tones, and the dimples and freckles were the same. It was the expression that had the most resemblance to Julian though; Julian had seen a million pictures of himself with that same grin on his face. "How come he left?"

Tristan smirked. "If you're curious, read it."

"He was friends with Theresa?"

"Yeah. It's kind of weird that she didn't talk about him to you, hey? Since she tells you so much about all the company dancers, you would think that she would have mentioned that she used to be really good friends with someone who was the fricking image of you."

Julian shrugged. "Not necessarily. Okay, I think I'm going to get this for River, it's on sale for eight bucks, and he'll like it."

Tristan read out the title. *"Bruno and Boots: This Can't Be Happening at Macdonald Hall!* Sounds ... great."

"It is," Julian said sincerely. "And — I think I'll get this, too. He picked up Theresa's biography. They went up to the counter, and Julian paid for the two books using a gift card his grandparents had got him for his birthday. As he put the two books in his bag, he had an uncomfortable thought. "Guys," he said as they started to walk back to the station, "do you think it is creepy to read the biography of someone you know? Like, isn't it kind of weird reading personal information about someone you know, stuff that they didn't tell you?"

Tristan sighed. "Jules, she probably thinks you have already read it. I mean, I've read it. You're probably like the only person at the academy who hasn't read it." Julian flushed, turning away from Tristan. Why was Tristan making him feel stupid all the time now? It wasn't his fault that he'd spent his childhood reading things other than dance biographies. Tristan hadn't even read the last Harry Potter book.

Kaitlyn Wardle
A parcel full of pointe shoes is the best mail ever! <3

"Mom? Where are my *pointe* shoes?" Kaitlyn was spinning frantically around her room, trying to see them.

"Which pair?" Cecelia called from the next room.

"The ones that I started to break in on Thursday, that I wanted to use for today."

Cecelia came into her bedroom, her arms filled with a huge pile of Kaitlyn's shoes. "I sewed a bunch last night, want to take these?"

"No! I need the other pair because they're broken in." She took the pile from her mother anyway and laid it on the bed, and then climbed under the bed, looking for the shoes.

"There's nothing under there, I cleaned your room yesterday," Cecelia said patiently.

"I can't find them," Kaitlyn wailed. "Oh, here they are." She grabbed them from on top of her desk, and picked up the pile of homework that she was supposed to finish for school on Monday. There was Sunday rehearsal to get through first, though.

"Kaitlyn."

"Yes?"

"Do you remember what we discussed? What are you going to do today?"

Kaitlyn sighed, sitting down on the bed to recite the list of stuff she had to do. "Ask Mrs. Demidovski if there is a chance of me getting Swanhilda back. Ask Mr. Moretti if I can start having privates with him again. Ask Gabriel to get me a letter of recommendation from one of the teachers of summer intensive auditions. Tell him that I am going to be missing class and rehearsal on Monday for summer-school auditions."

"Good." Cecelia leaned over and kissed her on the forehead. "Now hurry up. We have to leave in five minutes."

Kaitlyn walked into the hallway. There was something weird today. It was so quiet. Where was everyone? She walked downstairs to the change rooms, and straight into a gathering of everyone. They had all congregated in a group, huddled around the lost-and-found-box. There was Taylor, looking like she was going to giggle, and Julian, looking confused and asleep. Kageki was in the corner with his blank face on, the one that he put on when he didn't want to take sides. Keiko was beside Taylor, looking angry. There was Aiko, Leon, and Mao, looking hot and sweaty from their Youth Company practice, and Angela, looking horrified. There was Jonathon, looking half-angry, and half like he just wanted to laugh. Jessica was in the corner, looking even more furious than Keiko. Delilah was sitting beside them, looking like she was trying very hard not to laugh. And, there, in the centre, was Alexandra. "What's going on?" Kaitlyn asked, into the silence. The second she had walked in, they had all gone quiet.

"Grace," Leon answered briefly. Kaitlyn suddenly realized that Grace was the only one not there.

"What about Grace? Is she okay?"

"Yeah," Alexandra snorted. "Did you know that she has been paying the Demidovskis for roles? I was just telling Aiko about it, and then everyone showed up."

"Omigod, for real?"

"Yeah."

"Guys, I don't think that we should assume that this is true until we have confirmed it," Jessica interjected. "Like, how do you think Grace would feel about this? What if she didn't, or what if her parents didn't tell her about it?"

"Don't be annoying," Alexandra sighed. "It's real, okay?"

"How do you know?" Kaitlyn asked, sitting down on the floor. For something this big, she might as well be comfortable.

"I talked to her." Alexandra shrugged. "And, like, my mom knew because Gabriel told her by accident."

Taylor giggled, and Kaitlyn looked across the room, laughing with her. Of course Gabriel did. He had the special talent of almost always saying the thing that shouldn't be said to the person it shouldn't be said to.

"What did Grace say?" Aiko asked, her soft voice even quieter than normal. She looked more confused than anything. Aiko was so sweet, Kaitlyn thought to herself. She just worked harder than everyone else, and so she was the best, and because she was also older than them all, and Japanese, they left her alone. Next year and this spring and summer she was going to be auditioning, so she had been running on a lot less sleep and food than normal.

"Grace said that she didn't, but I know she was lying," Alexandra said firmly.

"How?" demanded Julian.

"Uh, she's my best friend, of course I know when she's lying," Alexandra said. She rolled her eyes. "She totally knows about it. I can't believe she's been lying about this for so long."

"It's almost one o'clock; we have to get to class!" Angela broke in. She stood up and went to get ready, everyone following her."

Kaitlyn followed Taylor to their lockers, and started to pull out her dance clothes. "Do you think it's true?"

"Yeah." Taylor nodded.

"I wonder if anyone else is." Kaitlyn frowned.

Taylor shrugged, pulling out her uniform with a grimace of displeasure. "Ugh, this uniform is so faded and stretched out now, I wish I could wear my new Yumiko, I ordered this really sweet one but it hasn't come yet — it's hot pink with turquoise edges."

"Sounds great," Kaitlyn lied. "So, what do you think this means for *Coppelia*? Like, do you think Grace will still get to do it, or what?"

Taylor shrugged. "I don't know, I guess it depends on how much the parents complain. Hey, do you wanna go to a party with me tonight?"

"What?"

"I can't bring Keiko, she doesn't drink. So, do you want to come? I won't actually be drinking, just a little bit. Come on, it'll be fun!"

"Um, I'll come, but I don't really drink." Kaitlyn had never drunk anything. Period. But it would be so exciting, and scary, to go with Taylor ... "Okay, I'll come. What should I wear? When?"

Taylor looked her over and frowned. "Um, why don't you come to my house after class and we'll find you some stuff? My mom will be cool with that, 'cause she wanted to grill you about which summer intensive auditions you were going to, anyway."

"Okay," Kaitlyn agreed. "Who is going to this thing?"

"Oh, nobody *you* know," Taylor assured her. "But it'll be fun!"

She walked off to get changed, and Kaitlyn slammed her locker door shut, closing the lock. *This should be interesting.*

Upstairs, everyone was still gossiping. Kaitlyn sat down at the side of the floor to put her *pointe* shoes on, basking in the comforting knowledge that they were all talking about someone other than her. It had been a difficult few weeks after she had not shown up to YAGP. Everyone had questioned her about "being sick" for ages, and she had gotten the impression that they didn't believe her story about getting pneumonia.

"Kaitlyn!" she heard someone whisper loudly from behind her. She turned around, frowning.

Her mother was in the doorway. Sighing, Kaitlyn stood up and walked over to her. "What?"

Cecelia grabbed her arm and pulled her out of the studio and behind the door. "I just found out something extremely interesting," she began.

"Grace has been paying for her parts?" Kaitlyn guessed.

Cecelia frowned. "You knew, and you didn't tell me?" she said.

"I just found out like five minutes ago," Kaitlyn explained.

"You should have phoned me."

"I was going to class! Can I go now?"

"No, you can't go! Do you realize what this means?"

"Grace is in trouble and the whole school hates her right now?".

"It means that we are going to get your part back! They can't keep you from playing Swanhilda when you clearly deserve it. I am going to go in there and give those people a piece of my mind."

"Mom, please don't," Kaitlyn groaned.

"I most certainly will! You deserve this role, Kaitlyn, and you are going to get it. It is unbelievable that the Demidovskis would let themselves be bought."

"Okay. Hey, can I sleep over at Taylor's tonight?"

"It's a school night."

"I know. Her mom can drive me to school tomorrow, and she can loan me some clothes."

"Are you sure that anything of Taylor's will fit you?" Cecelia asked.

"Yes! Seriously, Mom, stop it. She's got a few things that I've fit into before."

"What about your homework?"

"I'll do it with her."

"Yes, you and Taylor doing homework. That's a sight I'd pay to see. Especially considering that Taylor dropped out." Cecelia snorted. "Alright then, as long as it's okay with Charlize."

"Okay. I have to get back to rehearsal." Kaitlyn ran back into the studio and finished putting on her *pointe* shoes. They were perfect; softly molded to her feet, but still hard enough to provide enough support. She walked out into a clear space on the floor and began to *pirouette*, landing after four. She felt a little guilty for wasting such a perfect pair on class, they were so good that maybe she should save them for a performance. She *tendued* to the side and *ronds de jambed* to the back. Two *pirouettes* to start, and then she began to *fouette*, two normal, then one Italian, stretching her leg up to an almost 180-degree extension before rotating around into *attitude derrière*.

"Kaitlyn!" Gabriel gestured from the doorway. He looked frazzled, his hair sticking every which way. "Can you come here, please?"

Kaitlyn nodded and grabbed her stuff, leaving the rest of the dancers waiting for rehearsal. As she left, she checked the clock; almost eleven; they should have started by now.

"Kaitlyn, come here," Mrs. Demidovski said impatiently as Kaitlyn entered the office. Gabriel shut the door, and the office was suddenly isolated from the rest of the academy. Now there was just Kaitlyn and Cecelia, the Demidovskis, Mr. Moretti, and, of course, Gabriel, who was sitting behind his desk pretending he didn't exist. Kaitlyn wished that the floor would open and she would suddenly be out of here.

"Your mother tells me that you 'must' dance Swanhilda," Mr. Demidovski told Kaitlyn, his voice emphasizing the *must*.

Kaitlyn bit her lip.

"You want dance Swanhilda?" Mrs. Demidovski asked.

"Of course," Kaitlyn said automatically.

"Well, you aren't ready," Mrs. Demidovski said emphatically.

"Okay." It seemed the most diplomatic thing to say.

Cecelia glared at her before turning back to the Demidovskis. "You betrayed our trust by allowing a student to buy her way into roles that should rightfully be my daughter's," she said angrily.

"I think you are making a gross assumption here," Mr. Moretti said, leaning against the wall and looking at her, his eyes half-laughing. Kaitlyn blushed. She could tell that Mr. Moretti was making fun of her mother, and it embarrassed her. "You are assuming that the role would automatically be Kaitlyn's if it were not for Grace. Which is simply not true."

Kaitlyn was confused. She looked at her mother, who was opening and closing her mouth like a cartoon fish, and then at the Demidovskis, who were nodding their agreement with Mr. Moretti, suddenly looking a lot happier.

"Exactly!" Mr. Demidovski said, thumping one hand against his bony knee. "Kaitlyn, she, you, are not ready! Kaitlyn still has the childish mistakes, she is not enough developed. The tricks, very good, but the artistry, the details, not strong enough."

"Well, isn't that your fault as her teachers?" Cecelia asked, losing ground quickly.

"We have someone in mind as Swanhilda, and Kaitlyn is fine in the *corps*," Mrs. Demidovski said firmly. "She will make a good Friend if she works hard and listens to Mr. Moretti."

"But, Grace won't be playing Swanhilda?!" Cecelia protested.

"We will decide," Mr. Demidovski said firmly. To his left, Mr. Moretti nodded his agreement.

"Kaitlyn has to go to rehearsal," Mrs. Demidovski intervened. She looked at Kaitlyn. "Go, go, you will be late." Kaitlyn gratefully left the room, heading toward the studio.

Inside the studio, the usual prepared pre-rehearsal atmosphere had completely disintegrated. Everyone was sitting on the floor, giggling and gossiping. With Mr. Moretti busy in the office, rehearsal was already almost twenty minutes late in starting. Over in the corner, Kageki and Leon were making bets on how late it was going to be. "Definitely an hour," Leon said, shaking his head. "Mr. Demidovski's in there."

In the middle of the room, Tristan was attempting to do a lift with Alexandra, but they kept failing. Alexandra had red marks all over her back from Tristan narrowly grabbing her as she slid toward the ground. Jonathon stood up and walked toward them. "I bet I can do that with you," he dared Tristan.

"Yeah, right," Tristan scoffed. "You can try." He stepped into *arabesque*, and Jonathon lifted him straight up above his head, only his red face and the shaking of his biceps showing the effort it took for him to keep Tristan up there. He lowered Tristan down. "Nice man," Tristan said, surprised. "You've been working."

Jonathon grinned.

Kaitlyn stood near the *barre*, watching and laughing. It was so hilarious watching the boys try to partner each other; they were so competitive about it. Taylor walked up to her and leaned beside her on the *barre*. "What's going on?" she whispered.

Kaitlyn shrugged. "I don't really know," she lied.

"I hope we finish early so we can get ready," Taylor said impatiently, looking up at the clock. "It's almost twelve, and they still haven't even decided what order they are rehearsing. I thought we were supposed to be doing a full run-through today?"

"Who knows?" Kaitlyn walked away from Taylor, heading over to sit with Jessica and Keiko, who were doing some homework as they waited. Jessica was frowning over a page that had a lightly pencilled-in thought map. "I can't think of a good thesis," she complained.

"What's it supposed to be on?" Kaitlyn asked, sitting next to her.

"Whether I believe that changes in environmental policy originate with the public or institutions," Jessica moaned, burying her face in her hands. "This is so stupid."

"I thought you guys were working on *Macbeth*?" Kaitlyn asked, confused. "That's what Alexandra was working on."

"I failed the *Macbeth* test because I didn't read the stupid book because I was too busy with competition," Jessica complained. "So, now I have to do this stupid essay."

Angela was calmly going through her math work, working through the answers at a methodical pace. Kaitlyn looked over her shoulder. "Ew."

"What?"

"Grade eleven math looks gross."

"It's fine," Angela said calmly. "You just have to be confident in the basics."

Kaitlyn shuddered. She didn't have basics in math, she had sheer panic, and worry that hit her ten seconds before she had to complete a quiz as opposed to the night before.

Mr. Moretti walked in, and everyone was suddenly quiet, turning to look at him. Tristan hopped out of Jonathon's arms.

Mr. Moretti looked around to make sure that everyone was paying attention. "Okay," he said, "I will be rehearsing Friends, and then I will be rehearsing the village corps, first act, and then I will be rehearsing with Leon, Tristan, Kageki, and Julian. The rest of you may go."

Grace got up to leave with Aiko, but Mr. Moretti put up his hand to stop her. "Aiko, you may go," he said. "Grace, I want you to stay and learn this." Grace went back to the side, putting her bag down again. Mr. Moretti, paused, considering. "Grace, you learn Alexandra's role," he decided.

After rehearsal, Kaitlyn ran to get changed out of her sweaty dance clothes and undo her hair. "Ugh, my hair looks gross," she said despairingly, looking in the mirror. The sweat and gel had turned into a clumpy mess.

"We can fix it at my house, don't worry," Taylor said, laughing. "Come on." Kaitlyn started doing up her boots. "Oh, and one thing," Taylor said, looking around as her voice dropped, "my mom doesn't know that this is a party. She's still mad about me dropping out of school, so I said that we're going over to your friend's to do homework. That way she'll believe that it isn't a party."

"Wait, so she'll assume that it isn't a party if it's *my* friend's house?" Kaitlyn protested.

"Yes," Taylor said firmly. "Hurry!"

Charlize was already waiting at the side of the academy. Taylor and Kaitlyn quickly climbed in. "You girls are fast today," she commented, looking through the rear window to make sure she didn't squash any small pink-tutu-clad toddlers.

"Mmm," Taylor said, "Mom, what's for dinner?"

"I don't know," Charlize said, considering. "I suppose we could pick up pizza."

"Yeah! I want pizza. Can you get me the kind that's just got cheese on it, nothing else?"

"Sure," Charlize said, heading out of Vancouver toward the North Shore. "What kind do you want, Kaitlyn?"

Kaitlyn considered. She hadn't had pizza in a while. This was a weighty decision. "Um, can I get the Hawaiian?"

"Sure, that's what I like, too," Charlize agreed. They drove on, the lights starting to flicker on in the fading light.

Inside Taylor's house, Taylor practically pushed Kaitlyn up the stairs and into her room, leaving Charlize to go phone for pizza. She put her bag on her bed and began digging through her closet. Kaitlyn sat gingerly down on the pink bed. It was very squishy.

"How about this?" Taylor asked, reappearing with a tank top. It was white with black lace on the edges, and three small buttons down the front.

"That's so pretty!" Kaitlyn said, jumping up and holding it up to her in front of the mirror.

"Try it on," Taylor suggested.

Kaitlyn pulled it on, and looked again. *Oh.* "It's sort of too low."

"It looks fine to me, but whatever, I'll look for something else."

Taylor came out with an off-the-shoulder baby-blue top. "Here."

Kaitlyn pulled it on. It was a little small, especially in the arm holes, but it would do. "Yeah. I like this."

"Okay." Taylor kept digging until she found a deep purple off-the-shoulder top with rhinestone buttons on the front for herself, and changed her jeans. "Too bad I don't have any jeans you would fit into," she said, sighing. "Oh well."

Kaitlyn pretended she didn't hear that last comment.

Taylor began to do her hair and makeup, and Kaitlyn gingerly added a bit of eyeshadow and mascara. She knew how to do stage makeup, but everyday makeup was beyond her.

"Now, put this hoodie on over top," Taylor ordered.

Kaitlyn obeyed, zipping it up just in time to hear Charlize say: "Girls! The pizza's here!"

Zack's house was lit up in the dark, and Kaitlyn and Taylor couldn't stop giggling as they walked up to it from the bus stop. "Oh, Kaitlyn, how come we never really hang out?" Taylor asked, wrapping her arm around Kaitlyn's waist. "This is so much fun!"

They walked into the light, and Kaitlyn was surprised to see a woman she assumed was Zack's mother opening the door. There were parents who condoned underage drinking?

"Come in, girls, don't you look pretty," she gushed. "All the kids are in the basement, so if you want to go downstairs …" Kaitlyn realized that there were two parties going on, one upstairs with adults and their party below. She and Taylor took off their shoes and headed down.

Downstairs there was a pool table, a couch, and a lot of people. Kaitlyn didn't recognize anyone. "Is anyone here from McKinley?" she whispered to Taylor.

"A few people," Taylor whispered back. "Zack's friends with all the other tech-club kids who work backstage. I met a few of them when I danced at the assembly before the break, but I only really know Zack. He should have gone to King William's, the school I was supposed to go to, but he didn't want to go to the same school as his brother. So I guess all these other people are his old friends who go to King William's."

"How do you know Zack?" Kaitlyn asked. But Taylor was already walking in. She hooked her arm around Kaitlyn's, leading her in a weaving path toward the kitchen. She pulled two coolers out of her bag and handed one to Kaitlyn. "You owe me," she said, giggling.

"How did you even get these?" Kaitlyn whispered back.

"My mom always keeps a bunch in the fridge and she doesn't care when I take them. She says that it's better than me getting roofied."

"Your mom is so weird," Kaitlyn said, laughing. "Like seriously."

"No, it makes sense." Taylor opened her bottle and somehow managed to spill a bunch over her jeans. "Oh geez, now it looks like I peed myself," she giggled. "Come on; let's go say hi to Zack."

"Okay." Kaitlyn followed her, sipping slowly on her drink. It tasted a bit sweet, like juice. It made her feel warm, and nice, and sort of happy. She liked this party; everyone was smiling.

"Hey, Zack," Taylor said, walking up to a small boy sitting on the corner of a table, talking loudly to a small group of people who looked several years older than him. They looked very entertained. He turned around when he heard Taylor, and Kaitlyn recognized him. He had been in her math class once, and had never shut up, except when he was absent, which he had been for a third of last semester. Second semester he hadn't shown up at all; the rumour was that he'd had to finish the course online because he was failing. "You do acting, right? You played that possessed kid on *Superbly*

Unnatural." Her head felt heavier than normal.

He nodded, grinning. His hair was blond and just covered his ears, and he had a cheerful face. He was holding a can of beer and looked ridiculously pleased with himself, but he was so small that he could have passed for twelve, not fifteen. He was wearing a pale blue dress shirt, and it hung off of him. "The ballerinas," he said, a bit too cheerily. "So you made it!" He was only looking at Taylor, and she sat down on the arm of the couch that he was sitting on. Kaitlyn stood by awkwardly.

"Yeah," Taylor said, looking around. "I, like, know almost no one here. What's up with that?"

"You guys and Matt and some of the tech-club kids over there are the only people my age," he admitted. "Everyone else is in my brother's grade. He goes to King Will's."

"Yeah."

"I like your hair." Zack kept tapping his foot, and Kaitlyn couldn't stop herself from watching it.

"Thanks," Taylor said, smiling and tossing her hair. "Your house is pretty sweet."

"I know, right?" Zack gulped some of his beer. Beside Zack was a tall gangly boy with red hair, and Kaitlyn giggled as she saw him roll his eyes.

"You want me to show you around the house and stuff?" Zack asked. He sounded weirdly stiff.

Taylor giggled again. "Totally. You should show me that robot you made." They headed off, Zack casually putting his hand on Taylor's back as they walked.

"So." The red-headed boy nodded at Kaitlyn. "I like how they bothered to say 'bye' to us."

Kaitlyn nodded, smiling awkwardly. "I'm Kaitlyn." She stuck out her hand for him to shake, and they both started giggling at the weird formality of it.

"Matt. I go to McKinley, too — I'm in the tech club. Like, when the lights go on and stuff, that's me."

"Sweet."

"You're friends with Taylor?" he asked, sitting down on the couch next to her.

"Yeah."

"So, did Taylor tell you anything about me?"

Kaitlyn noticed that Matt was also searching the room with his eyes, presumably also looking for Taylor and Zack. "No," Kaitlyn answered. She swallowed more of her drink. She felt oddly comfortable in this strange house surrounded by people she didn't know who were mostly a lot older than her.

"Oh. Okay. Yeah, she's been around our booth a lot lately. Zack's been showing her the mikes and crap."

"Cool." Kaitlyn couldn't think of anything else to say, but she didn't really care. She felt weirdly comfortable on this couch.

"You want to go somewhere quieter?"

Kaitlyn considered. Now that she thought about it, the dubstep was getting on her nerves. "Sure."

"I know where we can go play some games," he said, standing up and picking up his beer. "Come on."

Kaitlyn followed him out of the living room and into somebody's bedroom. Matt handed her a control and showed her the basics of how to play the game, and Kaitlyn tried to look like she cared. She never played video games. The colours were so bright that they forced her eyes to focus in on them. She was trying to round the corner on a yellow path when she felt Matt's fingers on her thigh. She pretended to ignore it. He took the controller away from her and pressed his mouth on hers. It was wet, and smelled of beer and mint. She felt his tongue press against her lips, and she quickly pushed him away. "Um ..."

Matt shrugged. "I thought you wanted to."

"Uh ... no. Sorry." Kaitlyn quickly brushed her hair out of her face, trying to stop the blush that she knew was spreading across her face.

"Like, we don't have to do anything ... I mean, I just think you're pretty hot."

"Um, thanks." Kaitlyn picked up the controller. "You want to finish the game?"

Matt sighed. "Not really. But okay." They stayed there for the rest of the party, barely talking to each other and focusing on the game until Taylor finally came and found her.

"Were you guys doing this all night?" she asked, leaning against Zack. "Come on, Kaitlyn, we have to hurry up. Zack's mom is going to give us a ride home." She jumped onto the bed and blew into Kaitlyn's face. "Do I smell like I've been drinking?"

"Ew, no, you smell of really gross mint stuff."

"Good." Taylor hopped off the bed and Kaitlyn followed her, picking up her hoodie. They got in the car, Zack and Taylor giggling at nothing. Kaitlyn sat silently on the side, feeling awkward. She felt like she should finish the other half of her cooler, but she also thought it would look weird since they were going home now, so she casually stuffed it in one of the car cup holders and left it there. She felt strangely exhilarated. There were a lot of things to think about. *Somebody kissed me.* She smiled involuntarily. It wasn't how she'd pictured her first kiss, and she didn't exactly think that Matt was at all hot, but it was still pretty cool.

"Did you guys have fun?" Zack's mom asked too loudly as she headed up the hill to Taylor's house. It suddenly occurred to Kaitlyn that Zack's mom had probably been drinking, and her hands clutched onto the sides of her seat, worried. Her mom had told her a thousand times to never accept a ride from someone who was drunk, but what was she supposed to do if she was already in the car? And what was safer, being driven home by an adult who had been drinking, or bussing home at this time of the night?

Soon they were home, and Kaitlyn and Taylor climbed tiredly out of the car, Taylor still giggling. "Did you have fun?" Taylor asked as they walked the last few houses to Taylor's house.

"Was she drunk?" Kaitlyn asked, still surprised.

"Zack's mom? No, of course not, she was just a bit buzzed. Geez, don't worry so much, Kaitlyn."

Taylor seemed strangely annoyed with her, so Kaitlyn dropped it, filing the incident in her head as something that she really didn't need to tell her mother about. Taylor pushed open her front door, and they walked in, to the safe smell of Febreze, not alcohol.

Chapter Four

Taylor Audley
No I do not want to add u, wierd dude who I have
never met before. Stop sending me mesagas it maks
u look crazy

After they had dropped Kaitlyn off at McKinley, Charlize
drove herself and Taylor away from downtown, to a
section of the city Taylor was unfamiliar with; residential and well-gardened. "Where are you going?" Taylor
asked, confused. She looked at the car clock; she had
to be at class in an hour and a half. Ever since she had
started taking class with the Youth Company as well as
normal class, she started dance at nine.

"I just thought we could go for a drive," Charlize
said in her brightest, most fake, this-doesn't-mean-
anything voice.

Taylor groaned. "Mom, what? Seriously, what the
frick?"

"Don't you *dare* swear in front of me."

"Sorry."

Charlize turned off the radio. "Taylor, have you
considered what you are going to do if you don't
become a dancer?"

"Of course," Taylor said automatically.

"Well, what do you think you want to do?"

"I don't know."

Charlize sighed. Taylor began to feel uncomfortable. This was going to be one of those days where she was lectured no matter what she said. "Mom, it's okay, I have time. I can always go back to school; Mr. Briggs said that I could, remember? I just need some time off for now. Or I could act, or be a model. There's lots of things I think I'd be good at."

Charlize turned the car around, breaking several traffic laws as she did so, and began to head back downtown toward the academy. "Taylor, I just don't want you to get stuck. I want you to have options in your life, a backup plan."

"Well, what do you think I should do?" Taylor asked reasonably. "Besides go back to school," she added quickly.

Charlize was clearly prepared for this question. "I think your idea about trying acting and modelling is a very good one. You should start exploring your options. Taylor, you're a beautiful girl, I don't want you to limit yourself to dance."

"Okay." Taylor shrugged. "Like — what do you want me to do?"

"I booked you some time with a photographer. I want to get you some head shots, and then we'll see where it goes from there. Talk to some agents, see what our options are."

"Okay. Wait, but it won't interfere with dance, right? Like, I won't have to miss any dance for this? I'm really getting a lot better, Mom; Mrs. Demidovski even said that I was the other day."

"Of course," Charlize agreed. "I wouldn't force you to give up dance, not ever."

"Good." Taylor settled back into her seat, relieved.

"But if you did get an audition, I would expect you to go to that instead of class," Charlize added.

Taylor looked over at her mother, opened her mouth to say something, then closed it again. *At least she's not still going on and on about how I should go back to school — I'll just fight with her about missing class if it comes up.*

Charlize pulled up beside the academy, and Taylor hopped out. "Have a good day."

"I will." Taylor slammed the car door behind her and ran up the steps to the studio.

Someone called out, "Hey!" Taylor stopped and turned around, recognizing the voice but too surprised to hear it to be certain.

Behind her was Andrew Lui, a huge grin lighting up his face.

"Omigod, cool, you're here?" Taylor squeaked.

"Yeah." Andrew looked around the studio hallway and expelled a large breath. "Whew. What a trip, eh? This place looks exactly the same as it did when I left!" He looked back at her. "You don't, though! Did I say you could grow up?" He frowned at her, his eyes twinkling as he tried to keep a straight face, his hands on his hips. "You're supposed to be only this high." He held his hand out to the level of his hips.

Taylor giggled. "This is so cool that you're back, everyone is going to be so excited! How long are you going to stay? Are you going to take class?"

Andrew nodded. "Yeah, gonna take class for — um, about a week? Got some time off, thought that I would visit the family, and of course my dance family!" They started to walk down to the change rooms together, and Taylor realized that she was almost as tall as him now. It felt so cool to walk with someone whose picture was actually hanging up on the walls of the studio in multiple places, accompanied by descriptions of his various awards and recognitions. There was no question about it, Andrew Lui was one of Vancouver International Ballet Academy's most successful grads, and he knew it. He walked down the hall with a slight swagger, a grin on his face as he watched out for anyone else that he recognized. He paused in the middle of the hallway as a thought occurred to him. "Hey, how old are you now, kid?"

"Fifteen," Taylor giggled.

"Shouldn't you be at school? Or are you giving McKinley the ditch for the day?"

Taylor scrunched up her face, unsure as to how Andrew would react. "Actually, I sort of dropped out so I could take morning class and focus even more on dance."

Andrew tilted his head on one side as he considered. "Hm. The academy's changing; they never suggested that I should do that."

Taylor didn't bother correcting his assumption about who had suggested she drop out of school. She didn't want to tell Andrew that she had been failing all her courses. Instead she waited for his verdict on her decision.

"Well, good on you, kid," he said finally, and Taylor let out her breath. "Way to just go for it, no safety belts. How is McKinley, anyway? Come on, let me know all the gossip!"

Taylor followed him down the steps and into the boy's change room. She sat on the bench and swung her legs as she thought of what to tell him. "Mrs. Flowers is either lesbian or dating Mr. Fu, who's married — no one can decide which it is. Tristan asked Julian out, basically, and Julian just ignored him. Kaitlyn Wardle, that girl who used to always win stuff at competition? She's going here now. Her mom's fat."

Andrew laughed as he changed his shirt. "Okay, I really doubt that Mr. Fu and Mrs. Flowers are having an affair, they probably are just laughing their heads off in the staff room about you guys. Who is Julian? And yeah, I had a run-in with Kaitlyn Wardle's mother a few years ago, she kept trying to buddy up to me — I didn't like her at all. Kaitlyn was a good dancer, though. Is she still?"

Taylor shrugged. "Sort of. Like, her technique is good, but she never has any expression, and she doesn't have that great a body. Julian came to the academy this year; he's one year older than me, and from the Island, and he's really cute." Taylor covered her mouth automatically and turned around, checking to make sure that there was still only her and Andrew in the change room.

Andrew laughed. "Somebody got a little crush?" he teased.

"No!" Taylor said, blushing. "Oh! And I almost forgot! Me and Julian have been paired together a lot this year, and then for Spring Seminar, guess who was teaching?"

Andrew shrugged.

"Theresa Bachman. She really, really likes Julian, so she's been giving us privates ever since."

Andrew frowned. "Turn around," he ordered, "I have to change my pants."

Taylor obediently closed her eyes and turned to face the wall.

"There, done — okay, what? You and this Julian dude are having privates with Theresa Bachman? *The* Theresa Bachman?"

Taylor nodded, unable to contain her grin. "Yup."

"Children nowadays!" Andrew said, shaking his head in disbelief. "Why, when I was your age I counted myself lucky if Mr. Demidovski even looked at me! And here you are, having privates with Theresa Bachman. What is the world coming to?"

Taylor giggled. "We all watched that YouTube clip of you doing Golden Idol," she told him. "We got in trouble, because we were watching it on my laptop and we were supposed to be doing Social Studies stuff."

"Who's 'we'?"

"Me, and Kaitlyn, in class."

"Did you like it? Was I good?"

"Yes, of course! You were so awesome, and your jumps were so high, and Kaitlyn thought you were really cool."

"Thanks." Andrew grabbed his soft shoes out of his bag and swung the bag up on top of the lockers. He hit one in the middle that was covered in writing. "Who's got my old locker?"

Taylor hopped off the bench and went over to look. "I think that's Tristan's. Yeah, it is."

Andrew looked at it. "Got a Sharpie?"

Taylor thought. "No, but there's always one here —" she stood on the bench and felt around the top of Tristan's locker. "Here," she said proudly, hopping down and giving it to Andrew.

"Thanks." Andrew took off the cap of the marker and looked for the clearest space left on the locker. There was a small oval patch near the handle, so he began to draw a dancing figure, with stick arms and legs and a frilly tutu.

"Don't take up drawing."

Andrew put the cap back on the Sharpie and threw it up on top of the old lockers. "I'm gonna go and warm up — I guess you're in my class then, huh?"

Taylor nodded.

"Hmm." Andrew didn't look very thrilled with this. "See ya up there then." He went out, making an exceptional amount of noise on the stairs for such a graceful dancer. Taylor went to get changed and do her bun as the rest of the people in the Youth Company trickled in to get ready.

"Hey Aiko," Taylor said, smiling as she looked up at her. Aiko was the best dancer in the Youth Company according to popular opinion, including the Demidovskis', but she was also the nicest in Taylor's opinion.

"Hi, Taylor-*chan*. I like your bun, it is very *kawaii* today. Let me see?" Aiko stood up on her *demi-pointe* to look at the top of Taylor's bun. Taylor had twisted three coils of her hair separate from the rest of her bun and used them to create a pattern on the top before winding them around and tucking them under to join the rest of her hair. "Very nice! Maybe someday you do in my hair?"

"Yes." Taylor beamed. "Anytime you want, I'll do it for you, Aiko."

"Thank you, Taylor, you're so sweet." Aiko walked away to get changed, and Taylor hurried up. Aiko always had a spot at *barre* because people saved it for her, but she'd better hurry if she wanted a space with some leg room.

The studio was already full, but strangely quiet, different from the afternoon classes. Those that were talking were doing it in hushed voices, and the majority of the students were just quietly stretching, listening to their iPods. Taylor did the same, listening to Mat Kearney's cover of "Dancing in the Dark" as she began to stretch her legs. What was there about the morning that made everything seem so much less real? There wasn't enough light in the studio yet, so someone had turned the side lights on, but not the big overhead ones that they used for night rehearsals. Everything was soft and sleepy, and as Taylor stretched, she could feel her body wake up for the day. It felt so good to crack everything, stretch every muscle that was sore from yesterday, and have everything in her body come alive again. She pitied people who never used most of the muscles in their body and so never found out how good it felt to feel them all at once.

Dimitri came in, late as usual, and made a place for himself between Taylor and Mao, even though there wasn't really any room. Taylor ignored that and shifted a little closer to Aiko.

A bang of the door signalled the entrance of Mr. Yu, bringing energy and emotion into the half-awake room. Everybody started at the sudden noise, and slowly began to rise from their stretching positions, or take out their iPod headphones, or shed warm-up clothing. Taylor took off her down-filled warm-up boots and put her iPod inside them. "Very romantic," Mr. Yu said sarcastically, referring to the atmosphere. He flicked on the overhead lights.

Taylor winced, automatically covering her eyes from the harsh light.

Mr. Yu walked over to the *barre* and bent his back over it, cracking it with a sigh of relief. The sound of so many bones in his body cracking at once made a loud noise in the quiet room. "Good," Mr. Yu said. "Keep me young." He signalled to George, who was behind the piano already, and hummed the general tune that he wanted. George began to play something utterly different, and Mr. Yu began to give the first exercise: "And breathe. Rise uppppp …. And dowwwwwwn … and uuuuuppp … and hold." He looked over at Taylor and hit her in the butt. "Squeeze and rotate! Don't make soft!" He moved down the *barre*, handing out corrections verbally and physically. He didn't notice that Andrew was there until he had almost finished his round. Throughout the exercise, they'd all been sneaking glances over at Andrew, waiting for Mr. Yu to spot him. Mr. Yu stood beside Andrew, a frown on his face as he tried to comprehend what his former student was doing there. Andrew kept his head moving with his *port de bras,* his lip twitching with the effort to keep a straight face. "You!"

Andrew kept working, pretending not to hear, and then suddenly looked up, gave a fake start of surprise. "Mr. Yu! Didn't see you there!"

Mr. Yu started laughing, shaking his head. He gave Andrew a hug. "Long time no see," he said stiffly, the expression right but unnatural on his tongue. "How long you back?"

"A week."

"Then go back to work?"

"Yup."

Taylor could feel sweat begin to bead down her back by *tendues,* and she started to remove the last of her warm-up clothes. Mr. Yu snapped at Mao as she tried to rotate from an *arabesque* to a *develope devant.* "Why you still jerk?" he asked, referring to the hip shift she made as her leg moved from the back to the front. "How old you now?"

Mao looked up. "Seventeen."

"Too old! Too old have hip shift, way too old."

Taylor instinctively moved a bit back from Mao on the *barre* as Mr. Yu stayed close to them, watching Mao carefully. Taylor knew that he cared about how good Mao was more than he normally would because she homestayed with him. He didn't want anyone in his homestay to be doing badly.

Finally Mr. Yu snapped and yelled, "Stop!" across the room to George. George took his hands off the piano keys, raising his palms up in the classic gesture of surrender. As the last notes died away, Mr. Yu turned to Mao. "Why you no improve? Why you not better?"

Mao was quiet, confused.

Mr. Yu shook his head disgustedly. "If you not improve, why I teach? For fun? You still the same as when you come to Academy. Same mistakes." He looked at her. The whole class was watching them, some concerned, some entertained, some bored. "When you come to Canada from Japan?"

"When?" Mao asked, making sure of the question, nervousness making her English weak.

"Yes, when! What, you deaf, too?"

Mao shook her head.

"Do it again." Mao tried again, but made the same hip shift. Her muscles weren't strong enough to make it around smoothly. Mr. Yu expelled a breath of air, disgusted. "Get out."

Mao looked at him, confused.

Mr. Yu pointed at the door. "There door. Out. You don't listen, don't improve, go out, have fun. Go."

Mao stayed at the *barre*, not moving.

Mr. Yu glared at her. "Why you not go? Go!"

Mao didn't move.

"Okay, you no listen to me? Fine. I leave." He walked toward the door, and at the doorway he turned around, staring at the class. "Class finished. Thank Mao." He walked out the door.

Everyone stared at Mao, who looked like she was going to cry.

"Uh —" Andrew spoke up. Everyone turned to look at him. He turned to George. "Can I have some *frappe* music, George?" he asked.

George nodded and played a few chords. "That good for you, Andy?"

"Perfect." Andrew turned toward the *barre* and began directing a *frappe* exercise. "And one, two, three … and one, two three. Rise, *fondue*, out — *pirouette*! To the side. And one, two, three …"

Taylor looked over at Mao, standing in front of her. She was marking the exercise, watching Andrew carefully, and looked much calmer. Taylor began to learn the exercise.

After class, Taylor went downstairs to change into her uniform. As she came out of the stall, she saw Mao standing next to her locker, fumbling with the lock. She looked like she'd been crying. Taylor paused, waiting to see if she was all right. Mao looked up and saw her. "Oh! Taylor. I'm sorry for ruining class."

"You didn't ruin class, Mao," Taylor assured her. "I'm glad Andrew taught us. It was fun. Are you okay?"

Mao nodded, and quickly became very interested in searching for something in her locker, so Taylor left her and went upstairs.

Mr. Demidovski was sitting in the hallway watching a younger class practise, as he did occasionally. He had a small smile on his face, and kept glancing proudly over the lobby, like a king surveying his kingdom. "Taylor," he said, nodding at her. "How are youuuu?"

"Good," Taylor said, smiling. "How are you, Mr. Demidovski?"

"Look," Mr. Demidovski said, pointing through the open door to the studio. "See Michael, see Chloe — they are getting much better."

Taylor nodded, biting her lip as she watched. They weren't really that much younger than her, Michael was twelve and Chloe was eleven, and watching younger people that were better than she was at their age always made her feel a little sick. Mr. Demidovski lightly grabbed her arm and pulled her toward him. She leaned in. "Mr. Demidovski want you to learn Swanhilda," he whispered. He let her go and said in a normal voice, "Yes?"

Taylor nodded, very quickly. She was confused. Did this mean that he might be considering having her dance Swanhilda? That couldn't be true.

"Shush," Mr. Demidovski said, putting his finger to his lips. "Don't tell." He looked around the lobby at all the other dancers scattered around out of earshot, and then back at Taylor. He nodded meaningfully.

"Yes."

Mr. Demidovski got up with a fair bit of effort and walked slowly down the hall, back to the office. Taylor went to class, her brain buzzing with what he had said.

Taylor ran all the way from the bus stop up to her house,

and straight to her room. She opened up her laptop and carried it to her bed, going onto YouTube and searching "Swanhilda variation." Charlize came up to her room, confused. "Are you all right, Taylor? What happened?"

"I'm good," Taylor said impatiently.

"What are you doing?" Charlize asked, folding her arms.

"Watching Natalia Osipova do the *Coppelia* Act 1 variation," Taylor answered. "Okay?"

"Why was that so urgent that you couldn't be bothered taking off your shoes?"

Taylor looked away from her screen and down at her feet. *Uh oh.* "Um — today Mr. Demidovski said something very weird and strange, but maybe good?" Taylor muted the volume on the video.

"What did he say?"

"He said that he wanted me to learn Swanhilda." Taylor looked up at her mother, hoping that she would be able to illuminate Mr. Demidovski's vague statement.

She was out of luck. Charlize frowned and shook her head, just as confused. "What is that supposed to mean? Learn Swanhilda for what? For competition? Does he actually want you to rehearse it for *Coppelia* this year? What else did he say?"

Taylor shrugged. "That was it. I don't know what he meant. Oh, and then he told me not to tell anyone."

Charlize blinked. "That's not strange at all. What are you doing then?"

"I'm just going to try and learn all the Swanhilda variations tonight. I basically know them, but I want to *actually* know them."

Charlize shook her head. "Okay. That seems like a good idea. I don't know what else you could be doing. Dinner in an hour. And could you please get started on your online school work? I know Mr. Briggs told you to take a break from school, but that doesn't mean that you should be doing nothing. If you don't use your brain, it doesn't get developed, and you never get any smarter."

"Okay, okay," Taylor said, not listening. She kept her finger hovering over the mute button until Charlize had finished talking, and then started the video again from the beginning. Natalia was so great. *Okay, time to learn this.* She started going through it, stopping the video every few seconds to make sure she was doing it right. She hoped this was the right version; she thought it was, but she couldn't remember exactly which version Grace and Alexandra had been rehearsing.

Alison came in and sat in the bed. "What are you learning?"

"Swanhilda. Go away."

"Is that the one with the doll that the boy falls in love with and then they're all mean to the old man who makes the doll?"

"Yes."

Alison watched Taylor mark the steps in the small clear space in her room for a bit, keeping very quiet. "Taylor, you're pretty."

"Thanks." Taylor sighed. It was always a bit hard to learn things from YouTube, because it was like learning from a mirror image, so she had to keep going back to make sure she was going in the right direction.

"I wish I was as pretty as you."

Taylor stopped, shocked. "What?"

Alison shrugged, looking sad. "You look like Mom, and I look like Dad. I wish I looked like Mom instead."

Taylor jumped on the bed beside her sister, nearly knocking her laptop to the ground, and wrapped her arms around her. "Alison, I think you're pretty."

"All my friends say that you're prettier than me, and then they ask why I'm not pretty."

Taylor looked down at the back of her sister's head and hugged her. She didn't know what to say. "I'm not prettier than you," she said slowly, "we just look different."

"Okay," Alison said, moving out of Taylor's arms. She obviously didn't believe Taylor.

"Um, Ali, I really have to learn this for tomorrow."

"Okay, okay, I'll go." Alison jumped off the bed and left, closing Taylor's door behind her. Taylor drew a deep breath in and then exhaled. *Okay, focus, Taylor. Learn this.* She began going through the first part of the first act variation again.

Chapter Five

Alexandra Dunstan
Wanting to be someone else is a waste of the person
you are. Kurt Cobain <3

Alexandra sat on the living room floor, bodysuits laid
out around her.

Beth came hurrying through the hallway, passed
the open door, and then walked back. "What are you
doing, Alexandra?"

Alexandra looked up. "Going through my
bodysuits. I wanted to adjust a few of them." She
looked down at the wine-coloured one in her lap.
"I wanted to maybe sew this one in the front, put a
gather in?"

Beth looked around the room. "Could you please
do this in your room?"

"Uh, okay — why?"

"We have guests coming over." Beth looked toward
the door.

Alexandra began hurriedly gathering up the
bodysuits. "Okay. Who?"

"Justin's bringing his girlfriend over."

"Oh." Alexandra slowed down, gathering up her
bodysuits.

Beth came into the living room and sat down on the couch. "It's Anna."

"Anna?" Alexandra looked up a Beth, confused. "Her name is Anna?"

"Yes. He's dating Anna Valarao."

Alexandra stared at her mother, her mouth actually dropping from shock. "What? No! He cannot date Anna Valarao! That is not okay! You told him that it's not okay, right?"

"I can't tell him that, Alexandra," Beth said, annoyed. "He can decide on his own who he wants to date, and so far she seems to be good for him. She's better than that Bridget." The way Beth said "Bridget" made the name have twice the syllables it ought to have had, and gave it a significance normally reserved for the name "Jezebel."

"But it's Anna!"

Beth shrugged. "If it bothers you that much, then you can discuss it with Justin." She stood up. "But please move the bodysuits out of the living room."

Alexandra grabbed the bodysuits, ran up to her room and threw them on her bed, then ran to her brother's room and knocked on his door. Realizing he wasn't in his room, she called his cellphone.

"Lexi. What's up?"

"Are you dating Anna Valarao?"

"Uh — yes, I am … look, is that all you called to talk to me about, Lexi? Because this sort of isn't a good time …"

"You can't date her!" Alexandra said. Her voice sounded a lot louder and higher-pitched than she had intended it to.

"Um, Lexi, I'm hanging up now. By the way, she's right beside me, and she could hear that."

Alexandra lost the connection, and she set the phone down on her bed. This was terrible. This was worse than terrible, this was awful. She ran downstairs, cornering her mother in the kitchen. "Is she coming for dinner?"

"Yes. And no, you cannot skip dinner."

"That's not what I wanted to ask. Can I invite someone over?"

Beth considered. "I suppose that's fair. As long as you are polite." She rethought. "And as long as it isn't Tristan."

"Why not Tristan?!"

"I'm not stupid, Lexi. I do not want you and Tristan making that girl miserable while she is here. You need to put your differences aside. I think she might be good for Justin; he said that his GPA has gone up since he started dating her."

"Yeah, he *said*. Have you seen his transcript?"

Beth didn't bother answering Alexandra, instead focusing on the sauce she was making.

"Okay, fine. I'll invite someone else."

Alexandra went upstairs and went through her conversation list on her phone, trying to find someone who would make the night more bearable. *Jessica? Definitely not. Grace? Uh, obviously not. Taylor (ew), Kaitlyn, Mao, Aiko, Emily ... haven't hung out with her in, like, a year, would be too weird. Kageki, Keiko ...* She gave up and started to look through her phonebook, through the people that she'd never even texted. *Julian. Hmm.* She paused, considering. There wasn't that much time left to decide; it was already almost five o'clock. "Eeny, meeny, miny, moe ..." *Oh, whatever.* She picked up the phone and called Julian.

"Hey, Julian?"

"Hey, Lexi ... what's up?" Julian sounded confused, and Alexandra didn't blame him. She'd never called him before.

'Hey, I've got like a massive favour to ask you. This is going to sound really weird ..."

"Okay ..."

"You know Anna?"

"Um ..."

"Sorry, stupid question. She's decided to date my brother." Alexandra waited for Julian's reaction on the other end of the line. All she got was silence. "Julian?"

"Um, yeah — is this a good thing? Or a bad thing?"

"It's a bad thing!"

More silence. "Why?"

Alexandra held the phone away for herself for a moment. "Ugh!" She put the phone back up to her ear. "It just is. Anyway, I was wondering if you wanted to come to dinner. Anna's coming over, and I just know it's going to be super awkward."

"Things are only as awkward as you make them."

"Not helping, Julian. Can you come?"

"Um, tonight?"

"Yeah."

"Well, I've got some homework I really need to do, but ..."

"You can do it here. I'll go ask my mom if we can go pick you up. Phone you when we're at your house."

"Okay, do you even know where I live?"

"Of course. *Everyone* knows where Mr. Yu lives. Bye." Alexandra hung up on Julian and ran back downstairs to where her mother was. "Mom, can you please drive me to pick up Julian? He lives in Mr. Yu's homestay."

Beth stared at her. "Lexi, are you insane? Mr. Yu lives way too far away, and I am in the middle of cooking dinner!"

"Mom, please! Come on, you're letting Justin date Anna, and Julian can't bus here, it's way too far and the buses are stupid."

Justin appeared in the kitchen door. "So what are you planning now, oh crazy, rude, annoying, idiotic sister of mine?"

"I hate you, Justin." Alexandra turned back to her mother. "Please? If have to go to this stupid dinner, then I get to have someone over, too. It's not fair."

"Oh no, you don't," Justin interjected quickly. "You are not inviting Tristan over. I've heard you two talking about Anna together, and you're enough of a bitch on your own."

"Language, Justin," Beth said automatically, putting the chicken in the oven. "And I already told her she couldn't invite Tristan, don't worry. Now she wants me to drive all the way into Vancouver, to the east side, to pick up that new boy."

"Who?"

"Julian," Alexandra interrupted, her voice pitching into a whine. "You have to, Mom, otherwise it's not fair."

"I remember Julian," Justin said, thinking. "You know what? Go get your coat; I'll drive you to pick him up."

Alexandra stared at him. "Really?"

"Yes. I like him; he seemed like a good kid."

Alexandra ran to get her purse and coat, and then followed Justin to his car, getting in the passenger seat beside him. She wanted to say thanks, but it didn't seem appropriate, so instead she said, "Why do you have to date Anna?"

Justin whistled, annoyed. "I can't wait until you turn into a normal human being and start liking boys. I like Anna because she's cool, and funny, and hot." He reached out and turned on the radio, adjusting it to the Peak and beginning to sing along to the latest Mumford and Sons track.

Alexandra frowned. Justin could actually sing, and play the guitar, and she thought it was one of the coolest things about him. Actually, she thought her brother in general was pretty cool, so why did he have to be so stupid? "But why do you have to date someone from my school?" she demanded. "Like, are there not enough girls at UBC? Besides, don't you feel like a pedo?"

"Not particularly, no," Justin said dryly. "Look, I'm sorry, but you're overreacting. And she's only two years younger than me. Not even, a year and a half."

Alexandra leaned back in her chair, the better to sulk.

Justin sighed. "Look, Alexandra, just give it up, please? Could you once, just once, act like the world doesn't revolve around you? I really like her, okay? I don't want you being dramatic and difficult to ruin this." He looked over at her, giving her his best guilt-inducing expression.

Alexandra sighed. "Okay. Fine. But it won't last, she's horrible." They drove the rest of the way listening to the music and not talking.

Alexandra hopped out of the car and ran to the house, knocking on the door. "Hi, Mr. Yu," she said as he answered the door.

He stared down at her, confused. "What you want?"

"Is Julian here?"

"Julian!" Mr. Yu shouted back into the house. Julian hurried out. "Lexi wants you." Mr. Yu crossed his arms, waiting to hear what Alexandra wanted.

"Uh, I'm going to go over to her house for dinner," Julian explained awkwardly. "Okay?"

"Okay? Mrs. Yu has already made dinner. You no eat here, okay, but you tell us!"

"Sorry, Mr. Yu," Alexandra said. "That's my fault, I invited him late."

"Your fault? Okay, okay." Julian quickly put on his shoes and followed Alexandra out to Justin's car. Alexandra could feel Mr. Yu watching them curiously from the doorway.

Julian got in the back, and as soon as they had started to drive, he turned to Justin. "What's this about you dating Anna?"

"I am," Justin said firmly.

"Oh, cool." Julian relaxed back in his seat. "Love this radio station."

"Me, too," Justin agreed. They drove back to the Dunstan home.

As soon as they entered the house, Justin ditched them to go get changed, and Alexandra and Julian were left awkwardly looking at each other. "Uh — want to come up to my room?"

"Sure." Julian shrugged. They walked up the stairs and Alexandra pushed open the door of her room. "Holy frickin' crap!" Julian stepped into her room and began to turn around, trying to absorb what he saw.

"What?" asked Alexandra, worried by his shock.

"I have never seen so many ballet posters in my life!" Julian stepped up onto her bed without asking in order to get a better look at the posters. "Geez. Polina Semionova, Natalia Osipova and Ivan Vasiliev (I really like this one!), Bridgett Zehr, Irina Dvorovenko?"

Alexandra nodded. "Yup."

"Daniil Simkin, Tetsuya Kumakawa, Alina Cojocaru ..." Julian fell to the bed, giving up. "Too many."

"Since when do you know names of famous ballet dancers?" Alexandra asked, surprised. "You never seemed to know who anyone was before."

Julian shrugged. "Um, I've been reading Theresa Bachman's autobiography and she talks about a lot of other famous dancers. Plus, I guess I figured I should start learning who these people are, right? But I'm not sure I want them all up on my wall."

"Well, what *do* you have up on your wall?" Alexandra asked defensively.

Julian thought. "Stuff. A few ballet posters. But, like, a lot of different stuff."

"Well, I like my posters." Alexandra turned to her dresser and began to fix her eyeliner.

Julian looked around, trying to digest the room. "It's so clean."

Alexandra grimaced. "Does that mean yours isn't?"

"Uh —" Julian quickly changed the subject. "So, have you done your homework yet?"

"Mostly. I still have some more to finish." Alexandra reached for her pile of binders and textbooks, and Julian opened up his backpack. They arranged themselves on opposing sides of Alexandra's bed, and Alexandra started to work. Julian stared thoughtfully at his notebook, chewing on his pencil.

"You done the Social Studies assignment?" he asked suddenly.

Alexandra didn't bother looking up. "Yes."

"Can I look at it?"

"No."

"I came all the way out here for you, and I still don't know why. Please? I won't copy it; I just want to look at it."

"Fine!" Alexandra passed it to him.

Julian began reading it, his mouth forming the words as he read.

"Please stop that."

"Uh, okay ..."

"Alexandra, dinnertime!" Beth called from downstairs. Alexandra hopped up, going to the mirror and fixing her hair. "Okay." She took a deep breath in. "Come on, let's go."

Julian followed her out of her room, down the hall, to the dining room. Justin and Anna were sitting on the couch, waiting for dinner, and Anna looked up, seeming a bit nervous, as Alexandra and Julian walked into the room.

"What are you doing here, Julian?" Anna said, surprised to see him.

Julian shrugged. "Just hanging out."

"With Lexi?"

"No, the dog," Julian said with a straight face, petting the large golden retriever that had just padded into the living room. "Hey boy, good doggy-dog-dog."

Anna shook her head, confused. "Okay, whatever."

"Guys, come and eat," Beth called. They all went into the dining room. Emma was already sitting down, waiting for her dinner and Justin and Alexandra both sat down. Anna went into the kitchen to help Beth bring in the dishes. "Thank you, dear," Beth said, smiling at her. Justin quickly hopped up from his chair and began to help out, as well. Alexandra heaved a great sigh and rolled her eyes. Julian, who had been standing around, unsure of his role in this drama, sat down next to Alexandra. Emma rested her chin in her hands, staring off into space.

"What's up?" Julian asked Emma.

"Emma, Julian. Julian, my little sister Emma," Alexandra said in a monotone.

Emma turned to Julian, ignoring her sister. "I got second."

"Oh," said Julian. "That's pretty good still. In what?"

"A gymnastics competition. And no, it sucks, because I lost against my best friend, and now we aren't best friends."

"How come? What happened?"

"I was mad at her after the competition because she was being mean and rude, so I pushed her off a stone wall in the parking lot, and now her tooth's chipped, and Mom has to pay for the dentist and I have to pay Mom back for it." Emma sighed darkly.

"Ah," Julian said. Alexandra could see his mouth twitch as he tried not to giggle. "That sucks."

Alexandra started to grin despite herself, seeing the situation from Julian's point of view. "Oh, Emma …"

"Don't laugh at me!" Emma kicked Alexandra under the table, and Alexandra stopped laughing to glare at her.

Beth, Anna, and Justin came in with the dishes, and they all sat down. "Where's Dad?" Emma asked.

"He's in Seattle, working," Justin answered.

"Yes," Beth agreed. "Would you pass Anna the potatoes, Emma?"

Emma passed them silently. "Don't you dance with Lexi?" she asked.

Anna nodded. "Well, sort of," she amended. "I used to. Now I dance with a different school." She spoke with the sort of condescending voice that people who have never really been around kids use to talk to kids, and Emma's eyebrows rose with all of the disbelief that her eleven-year-old self was capable of. She looked across the table at her sister. Alexandra shrugged and nodded. *Even Emma gets how horrible she is. WTF, Justin …*

The dinner passed painfully slowly in Alexandra's opinion, and seemed to be entirely too dominated by Beth asking Anna questions, and Anna answering them in a way Alexandra found painful. To make matters worse, Beth kept glaring at Alexandra and signalling with her eyes for her to eat. By the end Alexandra wanted nothing more than to slap Anna, so she did the next best thing; grabbed Julian's arm and fled the downstairs, making for her room. "Shouldn't we help with the dishes?" Julian asked.

"Definitely not," Alexandra said firmly. "Here — I'm just going to be a moment, have to go and do something — can you sit here and do your homework? Or, here's my laptop, you can go on Facebook or whatever. Don't look at anything though."

"Um, okay …"

Alexandra left him in her room, closing the door carefully behind her, and fled to the upstairs bathroom. *Stupid, stupid, stupid Justin, ugh!* She peered at herself in the mirror, she was barely able to focus she was so upset. Her stomach stuck out. *Oh god …* She bent down and quickly threw up most of the night's meal, then brushed her teeth. She hurried, thinking of Julian in her room. He could really be doing almost anything. She didn't want him to dig through her desk and find her application forms for the Royal Ballet School, San Francisco Ballet School, or Jackie Kennedy Onassis School, or to look on her shelf and find the science quiz that she had forgotten to study for and gotten a 66 percent on, or anything else she couldn't remember that was embarrassing …

She walked out of the door fixing her ponytail, and didn't notice Julian in the dark hallway. "Hey," he said, his voice sounding loud in the silence of the upstairs.

"Agh!" Alexandra jumped.

Downstairs they could hear the sounds of dishes clattering together, and Beth's laughter.

"What are you doing here?" Alexandra asked quietly, once her heart rate had calmed down. "Is something wrong?"

Julian shrugged. "You tell me," he suggested.

"Okaaay then, nothing's wrong. Come on; let's go back to my room. I'll make Justin drive you back home after Anna has finished sucking up to my mother a little more."

Julian followed her to her bedroom, and sat down on the bed. "You want to maybe tell me about what just happened?"

"No, I don't," Alexandra snapped. "Nothing happened." She picked up her homework and held it to her, suddenly fascinated with her search for a paper somewhere in the pile.

Julian chose his next words carefully. "Look — I'm not trying to be judgmental here. Or to accuse you of anything, or to help you. Honestly? I don't care what you do. I'm just sort of ... curious."

Alexandra sat next to him on the bed. "You're curious?" *I don't care if he knows, not really, not if he doesn't care and he doesn't tell anyone.*

"Yes," said Julian.

Alexandra's face suddenly lit up. "Jules, in your grade seven, was everyone always obsessed with Truth or Dare?"

"Yeah," Julian laughed. "I always picked dare."

"Let's play right now. Except, the person asking gets to pick truth or dare."

Julian paused, considering. "All right. But no cheating."

"Deal." They turned to face each other on the bed, cross-legged with their hands palms up and resting on their knees like they were about to meditate.

Alexandra giggled nervously. "Who goes first?"

"Rock, Paper, Scissors."

"Okay," Alexandra agreed. They poised their fists and counted to three before throwing. Alexandra chose scissors and Julian opted for paper.

"I lose," Julian said good-naturedly.

"Best out of three?"

"No, go ahead."

Alexandra scrunched her eyes shut, trying to think of the perfect question. Suddenly her eyes flew open. "Got it. Are you gay or straight?"

Julian's mouth flew open. "Out of all the things you could ask me, that's the one that you were most curious about?"

Alexandra shrugged. "Well, not exactly me. But certain people would really like to know."

Julian grimaced. "Tristan?"

"You got it." Julian bit his lip, wavering. Alexandra was confused. "Dude, what's the big deal? Nobody really cares. It's not like we're gonna hate you no matter which one you pick. I'll even promise not to tell anyone if you want." Alexandra subtly crossed her fingers as she tucked her left hand under her pillow. *I have to tell Tristan if I find out.*

"It's just —" Julian was strangely at loss for words. "I don't know!"

Alexandra blinked. "What do you mean? How can you not know?"

Julian shrugged. "How are you supposed to know, anyway? But I don't want to date Tristan."

"Okay." Alexandra thought. She thought so hard that she forgot to worry about what she had to answer next. "You really don't know, though?"

"No." Julian considered. "Do you think that means that I'm gay?"

Alexandra shrugged. "No, I think you just don't like anyone yet. I guess you'll find out when you find out. Until then, you'll just have to be the mandatory straight dude."

"What?"

"Well, you know how like on a TV show they'll stick a non-Caucasian actor on to look ethnic, or a gay guy to look accepting? In dance, almost everyone is a girl or gay, so the shows always have a mandatory straight guy. That's you. Me and Grace decided that ages ago."

"Um — thanks?"

"You're welcome." *I can't wait to tell Tristan this.* "Okay, now you Truth or Dare me, quickly before I get nervous." Alexandra closed her eyes in preparation.

"Truth. How come you throw up?"

Alexandra's eyes flew open, annoyed. "I thought that you were going to ask me *if* I threw up."

"I already know you do," Julian said, shrugging.

"Why do you smoke weed?"

"It's not your turn."

"I'm trying to explain. Answer my question."

"I dunno, because I like to. It calms me down."

"That's why I throw up."

"That doesn't make any sense."

"It doesn't have to."

Julian considered the logic of this. "I suppose it doesn't." He leaned back against the wall. "This is a strange night."

"Yeah," Alexandra agreed, grabbing her pillow and clutching it to her. She rested her chin on it. "I'm glad you came, though."

"Me, too."

"You won't tell anyone, will you?" Alexandra asked, realizing that this was a belated request.

Julian grinned at her. He shrugged. "Oh, I don't know —"

"Julian!"

"Okay, okay, I won't! Besides," he added seriously, "anyone who actually wanted to know probably already knows."

Alexandra decided to ignore this comment. She yawned. "We should do some homework."

Julian nodded. "Yeah." They both sat up and started to work.

Alexandra heard Justin wake Julian up and Julian say goodbye to her in the hazy space between sleep and consciousness. As she heard her door close, and the boys moving downstairs, she managed to climb under the covers. She slid into a deep, dreamless sleep a second after she managed this feat, but as she was trying to find the edge of the quilt, she wondered what Julian had thought she was going to ask him. *What other question could he have thought I was going to ask if it wasn't whether he was gay or straight?*

Chapter Six

Julian Reese
The Vaccines just released a new album! So stoked ... Is this how 13 year old girls feel about One Direction?

"Don't fall!"

Julian ignored the shouts below him. He swung on top of the thin metal barrier that blocked him from the ground, and slowly straightened to standing.

"Julian, you idiot ..." a girl shouted.

Julian kept his focus. Over to his left was the ledge he had to reach. He inched along the thin rail, not looking down. *There.* He reached over and grabbed the soccer ball, tucking it in his arm and going back, slowly, but more confidently. He jumped down and turned to a boy he knew slightly, but couldn't remember his name. "You owe me five bucks."

They traded the ball for money, and Julian started to walk off to class. "Julian! Julian Reese!" Julian turned slowly toward his counsellor's voice, a sheepish grin on his face. "Hi, Mr. Briggs."

Mr. Briggs was walking toward him, looking more frazzled than normal. "Julian. Glad I found you."

Julian frowned. Evidently Mr. Briggs *hadn't* just seen his stunt. "What's up, Mr. Briggs?"

"Your father wants you."

Julian was confused. "My dad's here? Like, in Vancouver?"

"He's in my office. Come on." Julian followed Mr. Briggs to the counselling offices, his mind a blank on what his father could want. Will was supposed to be on the Island. He hadn't told Julian that he was going to be in Vancouver.

Will was sitting in the counsellor's office, looking like he had slept in the clothes he had on. His hair was messy and slightly matted in the way that looked normal on Valdez but not so much in Vancouver. "Here he is, Will," Mr. Briggs said. "Let me know if you need anything else."

Will nodded, ignoring him. Mr. Briggs looked at him, obviously curious about the parent he'd probably seen the least of out of all the students that he was in charge of, but he walked off, giving them their privacy. "Hey," Julian said, questioningly.

"Hey. Look, just wanted to let you know, I'm going up to Kamloops for a few weeks," Will said.

"Okay?"

"So, I won't be able to watch your show."

"That's okay." Julian shrugged. "I don't dance much in it, anyway."

"How come?"

"I don't know. I'm not good enough yet?"

"Oh." Will paused, working up to what he had really meant to say. "So, has your mom talked to you yet about whether she's going to pay for your lessons yet?"

"I told you," Julian said impatiently. "She isn't paying for my lessons. I'm on scholarship, I just need my home-stay fees paid, and Luigi isn't going to pay for them since he and mom split up."

Will thought about this. "Well, could you ask him to?"

"Uh, no?" Julian said indignantly. "I am not going to ask him to do that! Why would he pay for my homestay if he's not dating Satya anymore?"

"Well, you could still ask him, Julian. So, does this mean that you will be home next year?"

Julian shrugged. "I don't know."

"What are your options?"

"I don't know! I'll handle it, Dad, I promise. I'll tell you when I know what I'm doing; I just really don't know what I am doing right now."

"Okay." Will stood up, stretching. "Ahhh, that feels good. Daisy's been getting me into yoga, it's great."

"Cool," Julian said, distracted by thoughts of what he was going to do next year. *Why do I always have to be the grown-up?*

"It was nice to see you, buddy. You look good."

"Thanks." Julian smiled. "You have to go now?"

"Yeah, a guy's giving me a ride up in half an hour; have to go meet him at the Canada Line Station."

"Kk, bye." Julian hugged him, and then Will left. Julian picked up his backpack and went to leave, going to his next class; but he was stopped by Mr. Briggs in the hallway.

"How is everything, Jules?"

"Pretty good."

"Everything working out for you? How are your classes?"

"Okay. Getting a B average, I think."

"Still like dance?"

"Of course!"

Mr. Briggs laughed. "Okay, just asking. That's my job, you know." He disappeared into his office with a large pile of McKinley school T-shirts, whistling the "Phantom of the Opera."

Julian walked out into the hallway and realized that his class must have already started; the main floor was empty. He broke into a run, up three flights of stairs until he ended up in his Biology class. He slid onto a chair next to Tristan.

Mr. Fu was already writing on the board. "Now, the translation step in protein synthesis has three mini steps," he said over-excitedly as he drew on the white board. "These are *initiation*, *elongation*, and *termination*."

Julian reached in his backpack, pulling out his notebook and writing the notes down. "Hey, can I copy what I missed?" he whispered to Tristan.

Tristan pretended not to hear him and Julian frowned. He could see Tristan's notebook, and it had a full paragraph of writing in Tristan's peculiarly small and neat printing. "Tristan! Can I copy?" He looked up; Mr. Fu was drawing pictures of DNA strands untangling, and he looked like he was going to be a while.

"Fine!" Tristan muttered. "You can copy after class!"

Julian frowned. The writing was right in front of him. If Tristan would just move his elbow to the side a little bit, he could read it … there, if he leaned at an angle he could get it. He began to write in his own loopy printing: "DNA is transcribed to mRNA in the nucleus and mRNA is translated into protein in the cytoplasm …" Julian wondered why Tristan was in such an annoying mood lately. He had been so much fun at the beginning of the year, and now he was always grumpy and never seemed to have any time for Julian.

After class, Julian stopped to drink from the water fountain. "Hey, Julian," Jonathon said. "How's it going?"

Julian stood up and wiped the water from his mouth. "Good." They began to walk to the bus stop, weaving through the usual lunchtime chaos.

"I heard that you were going to be in Leah's new piece."

"Yeah!" Julian grinned, suddenly remembering. "Yeah, I am." A list had appeared on the academy schedule board yesterday morning. It had been titled "Contemporary June Piece" and the teacher listed had been Leah. There had been a rather small list of dancers on the list, and Julian was stoked to be included. "You?" Julian actually couldn't remember if Jonathon had been on the list or not.

"Nope." Jonathon shrugged. "Whatever. Contemporary's not my strong suit."

Julian frowned. He flashed back to the many conversations that he had had with Jonathon. "I thought that you said you used to always get first place in any contemporary competitions that you had? And remember you said there was that girl who was in love with you because of that contemporary piece you did where you were almost naked? And what about that contemporary teacher who told you that you should stick to contemporary because you were too expressive for ballet?"

"Uh," Jonathon said, swiftly backtracking, "yes, but that was different contemporary. That was proper contemporary. Leah's is more like jazz."

"Well, I like Leah's contemporary," Julian said loyally.

"Mmf," Jonathon answered.

"How are privates with Kaitlyn going?" Julian asked curiously.

"Oh. I decided not to ask her if she wanted to share privates," Jonathon said quickly.

Julian was confused. "But I thought you were going to do it last Friday. Remember, you left me and you were totally going over to her to ask?"

"I changed my mind," Jonathon said briefly.

Julian stopped asking questions and they walked to the bus stop in silence. Julian was beginning to doubt that Jonathon had actually accomplished all the feats that he bragged about.

The bus was late as usual, and Julian made his way to a seat beside Tristan and Delilah. They were both absorbed in whatever they were talking about with each other, so Julian put on his iPod and listened to his favourite Gotye song as he began to eat his lunch.

Inside the studio, Julian was excited to learn the piece. They were all sprawled out on the floor, waiting for Leah to arrive. So far, there was Julian, Kageki, Michael, Delilah, Taylor, and Chloe. Three boys and three girls. Michael and Chloe looked both terrified and ecstatic to be in the same piece as the other four. Taylor looked exhausted and sweaty. "How was morning class?" Julian asked her. "Still fun?"

Taylor nodded, smothering a yawn. "So tired. Mrs. Castillo had us doing *petit allegro* for an hour straight, I swear. And then an hour of *grande allegro*." Her bodysuit was soaking wet in the back and the front, and as she rolled away from a spot on the floor that she had been lying on, Julian could see a damp spot from her sweat. Kageki was busy doing *pirouettes. Around and around and around* — Julian watched him turn, envious of his confidence.

Leah walked in a bit late, and flung her bags to the row of seats beside the mirror. "You all here?" She did a head count. "Okay, good. Now, I had wanted Alexandra and Tristan to be here too, but the Demidovskis tell me this is impossible —" Leah shook her head, annoyed. "So, it's just going to be the six of you." She sat on the floor, stretching her legs out in a *V* in front of her. "So, let me tell you what's going on. This piece is going to be awesome. Who's heard the song 'Somebody That I Used To Know?' The Gotye song? Julian flung his hand out, a huge grin on his face. He'd just been listening to it on the bus! *We're doing a piece to that song? Oh, please, please!*

Leah looked around. "Just Julian?" She sounded surprised.

Taylor rolled over to Julian. "Is that the one that you made me listen to?" she whispered. Julian nodded, and Taylor put her hand up.

"Two people? Okay, that's better."

Beside Julian, Michael looked upset, like it was the first day of a class and he was already failing.

"It's okay if you haven't heard it already," Leah said. "That's your homework. I want you to go watch the music video on YouTube tonight. The piece we're doing today is going to be choreographed to that song. Now, I'm just going to partner you guys up: Michael and Chloe, Julian and Taylor, Kageki and Delilah."

They nodded. They'd already been sitting in those pairs, assuming that she would sort them this way.

"Now, I want you to listen to me," Leah said, leaning forward and looking them in the eyes. She was talking to them seriously, as if they were co-conspirators, not a teacher and her students. "The reason that we are starting rehearsal on this piece so late is because the Demidovskis wouldn't give me the time or the studio space with you guys. This piece is going to be given last priority, after *Coppelia*. I need you guys to make it your first priority, all right? If I say come, rehearse, I want you to come. No 'Oh, Mr. Moretti wants me to rehearse Villagers for another six hours,' no 'Oh, Mrs. Demidovski just wants me to stand here modelling this costume for her for the next hour.' Do you understand?"

They nodded.

"Good. This piece *should* be your first priority. Mrs. Demidovski told me that you are all in the *corps* of *Coppelia*, so there should be no problem."

Julian saw Taylor gulp and look down beside him. He frowned; what did that mean? Had she been given another role recently? He thought that Mao and Keiko were first and second cast of the flower *pas de deux*.

"Let's get started." Leah walked over to plug her iPod into her player, and the dancers began to take off their sweatshirts. Julian grinned at Taylor; this piece was going to be so much fun.

After they had been rehearsing for an hour and a half, the door opened. Mrs. Demidovski walked in with Mrs. Castillo. "May we watch?" Mrs. Demidovski asked. It was not a question.

"They haven't learned much yet," Leah protested.

Mrs. Demidovski waved away Leah's objections. "Just show me."

"All right." Leah sighed. "Everyone, from the beginning. Don't worry if you forget something." She turned on the music, and they began.

After about two minutes, the piece had completely unravelled. Leah stood up and began marking the girls' part for them, but as the girls tried to copy her, the boys were utterly lost. "All right, enough." Mrs. Demidovski put her hand up. "Good." From the tone of her voice Julian could tell that she meant the opposite. "Good. Thank you." She turned to Leah. "I will send Cromwell Gilly up to you, he can show you which costumes you can use in the costume room. Taylor, Jules, with me." Taylor and Julian immediately stepped toward her to follow her from the room.

"Hey," Leah protested. "Can I please have them for a bit more? We're still working here."

"They can catch up later," Mrs. Demidovski assured her. "They need to rehearse *Coppelia* right now." Taylor and Julian followed Mrs. Demidovski out of the studio, heading downstairs and leaving an extremely frustrated Leah behind them. Julian fought not to giggle; on one hand he could sympathize with Leah's difficulties in dealing with the Demidovskis, but on the other hand it was extremely entertaining to watch Mrs. Demidovski so easily win an argument with her.

Downstairs, it was sunny and everyone who hadn't been on the list for contemporary was in the big studio, rehearsing first act. Julian went to walk in the studio, but Mrs. Demidovski grabbed him by the shoulder and pulled him back. "Come here," she insisted, leading Taylor and Julian into studio B instead. Julian looked at Taylor and she shrugged.

Inside studio B, Theresa was waiting. "Hi," Julian said, even more confused. *Why is she here?*

"Mr. Demidovski wants Taylor to learn Swanhilda," Mrs. Demidovski explained. "I don't have time to teach. Julian, you are already an understudy for Frantz, you can rehearse with Taylor. Theresa will help you." Mrs. Demidovski nodded to Theresa and then walked out.

Julian turned to Theresa. "Does this mean that you are a teacher at the academy now?" he asked, confused.

She shook her head and shrugged. "They're paying me, I hope," she answered. "I think she said that the teacher who is in charge of rehearsing *Coppelia* doesn't want Taylor to be rehearsing *Coppelia* …?"

"Mr. Moretti," Taylor and Julian said together.

"Ah. Mr. Moretti." Theresa's tone was not one of carelessness, but one that was begging to be asked questions.

"What about Mr. Moretti?" Taylor obliged.

"I knew him a long time ago, that is all. Now, come on, let's rehearse, you have a lot of work to do." Theresa began to teach Taylor her part, and Julian sat down cross-legged on the floor, staring wistfully up at the ceiling. He could hear the Gotye music, and he wanted so badly to be upstairs.

The door opened, and Charlize poked her head inside. "Hi, everyone," she said happily.

"This is not a private," Theresa said quickly. "This is a rehearsal. I'm sorry, but I need you to go."

Charlize ignored her. "Taylor! I need you to come, right now. You have an audition in an hour."

"What?" Theresa protested. "What do you mean? Audition for what? She's rehearsing for Swanhilda, she can't go right now."

"They're looking for boys, too, Julian," Charlize said, nodding to him. "I think it might be an open call — it's for ballet-trained dancers. You should come along, too, we'll see if we can get you in."

"They can't leave!" Theresa said angrily. "I don't think you appreciate that —"

Charlize raised her impeccably plucked eyebrows. "I don't think that you appreciate that Taylor is my daughter. I decide what she has to do, not you. Taylor, go get changed."

Taylor picked up her bag and water bottle and left the room. After a second's wavering, Julian did the same.

"Your mother's scary when she's angry," Julian said, following Taylor to the girl's washroom. Taylor started to take off her bodysuit, and Julian quickly turned away. He had noticed that Taylor had started treating him like he was gay, and he wasn't entirely sure how he felt about it. Confused, mostly.

"Yeah, that's all the time lately," Taylor said, pulling on her shirt and starting to pull the sparkly pins out of her hair. "Daddy's getting married again. Mom's all pissed because she says that she's a gold digger."

"Does your mom still miss him?" Julian asked, pulling his jeans over top of his ballet shorts.

"I don't think so," Taylor answered. "They divorced when I was twelve, and my mom always says that the only good thing to come out of that marriage was me and Alison."

They went upstairs and joined Charlize. "You don't have head shots, do you, Julian?" Charlize asked rhetorically. "Don't worry about it. Now, it's just a small audition for *Superbly Unnatural*. They need a ballet dancer and a contemporary/hip hop dancer, and that's all that the breakdown said."

"Okay," Julian shrugged. "I guess I'll just go in and do whatever they ask me to?"

"Exactly," Charlize said, beaming at him.

"Mom," Taylor said from the front seat. She'd been sulking for the last five minutes and was annoyed that nobody had noticed yet.

"Yes, Taylor? What's your problem now?"

"Theresa was in the middle of teaching me Swanhilda," Taylor said. "Mrs. Demidovski wanted me to learn it. Now what?"

"Oh," Charlize said. "That is very unfortunate." They pulled up to the gates of the studio, and Charlize drove past the security guard. "It says Building C ... Okay, here. Come on guys, you have fifteen minutes." They piled out, and Julian followed Taylor up the steps. This was turning out to be one of those days where he just didn't know what was going on, and Julian was at his happiest when he could just go with the flow and plead no forewarning. *I'm going to an audition! This year just keeps getting more interesting.*

"Name?" the bored-looking girl at the desk asked. Julian stared at her makeup, wondering what it would feel like to have that much on. She had a pale complexion, but her foundation darkened her skin by at least four shades, and the blush over top was a shade of orange that no human being had ever produced in their cheeks before.

"This is Taylor Audley," Charlize spoke for them, "and this is Julian Reese, he's not on the list, but we were wondering if we could get him in, as well?"

The girl stared at them blankly. "I'll have to ask some-body about that. Here, fill out this form." She handed them two sheets, and they sat down to fill them out.

"I don't know any of this," Julian whispered, staring at his sheet. "What do they need all this information for?"

Charlize reached over, taking the sheet from him. He had filled in his name, cellphone number, height, and weight, but everything else was blank. Charlize looked worried. "Okay, I'll just put our address on it for you and sign it as your guardian — you have no idea what your measurements are?"

"No. Cromwell Gilly probably does, though ..."

"I don't have his number. Okay, just leave it blank then."
Julian nodded.

The girl came back and looked over at them. "They think that it might be okay," she said unenthusiastically. "So you can go in." She took Julian's single sheet and Taylor's sheet, resumé, and headshot.

Julian looked around the small room, confused. He had thought it would be full of dancers, since this was a dance audition, but nobody looked like a proper dancer. Taylor went over to the girl at the desk. "Do you know if we need to wear *pointe* shoes?"

"Uh —" the girl stared at her. "I don't know what *pointe* shoes are — are those like dance shoes?"

"The kind of shoes that you wear so that you can stand up on your toe," Taylor explained patiently.

"Oooh, toe shoes," the girl said, understanding.

"*Pointe* shoes," Taylor corrected.

"Whatever. I don't know, it probably doesn't matter. I don't think that anyone is wearing them, so whatever you want …"

Taylor went back. "I'm just going to put them on," she said, shaking her head. "It can't hurt, and I can always take them off."

"Taylor Audley?" Taylor hopped up and went into the room. Julian stared after her, starting to get nervous. He had no idea what to expect. In a few minutes Taylor was out again.

"That was really fast," Julian said, surprised.

Taylor shrugged. "Acting auditions are way different than ballet auditions," she said. "Like, they don't care about everything, so they don't need you to stay and take class for two hours. The lady just told me to do whatever I wanted for a few minutes, and there was no music. I did an *arabesque* and some *fouettes*."

"So weird."

"Julian Reese." Julian got up and walked into the room, resisting the urge to nervously twist his hands.

"Julian?" The lady behind the desk smiled at him. "How are you?"

"Good."

"Okay then, now what we're doing here is pretty straightforward: there are two dancers, a hip-hop dancer, and a ballet dancer, and they're rehearsing really late at night and things start to get crazy."

"Okay."

"So, are you a ballet dancer or a hip-hop dancer?"

"Ballet."

"Can you do hip hop? You said on your form that you've been dancing for quite a while, so you should be able to do hip hop, right?"

"Er —" Julian felt lost in the face of such irrational logic. "I can definitely try if you want."

"Okay then. When you're ready."

Julian stood there, waiting for some further instruction. "So like — just start dancing hip hop? Now?"

"Yes."

Julian started to dance what little he could recall of the few hip hop moves he had learned, feeling incredibly awkward doing it to no music. He was very close to the table where the people watching him were. It felt very odd to be trying to do hip hop in ballet clothing and shoes. After a few seconds he gave up and just stepped into a *pirouette* and then slid into the splits, grinning. He stood up.

"Thank you for coming out."

"Thanks," Julian replied, then left the room.

"How was it?" Charlize asked as they left the audition area.

"I have no idea," Julian said honestly. "I think that might be one of the weirdest things I have ever done in my life, and I have done some pretty weird stuff. Did I ever tell you guys about the time when I was little when my mom took me to one of her Wicca Womyn's gatherings and they were all dancing naked under the full moon?"

"No," Charlize said, laughing. "Don't tell me that was less weird than this."

"Okay, maybe not," Julian conceded. "But it was coming up pretty close. I was doing hip hop in ballet shorts and ballet shoes, to no music."

"Was it fun, though?"

Julian thought, and then he began to grin. "Yeah, it kinda was," he decided. "It *was* fun." They got in the car and drove back to the academy.

Theresa accosted them as soon as they got in the doors of the academy. "Quickly, quickly," she said. "There's a space free upstairs. Come on, Mrs. Demidovski wants to see it soon." They ran upstairs and into the small empty studio.

"Were you waiting for us this whole time, Theresa?" Julian asked, surprised.

"Of course," Theresa said, sounding shocked that they had supposed that she wouldn't. "I want you two to get this. Now, Taylor, come here. We are going to have to work very fast. You are going to have to be very smart for me, all right, princess? From here, no! Your hand goes here — Julian, can you be a love and run the CD player for me?"

In an all too short amount of time, they had to go downstairs and join the large rehearsal. Mrs. Demidovski came up to them, looking worried. "You ready? You are going to be good?"

"Yes," Taylor said, sounding more confident than she felt.

"Good. Don't let Mrs. Demidovski down." They walked into the room, and immediately could feel the sweat, so thick in the air that Julian could picture them being in Borneo. He wondered what kind of dances they had in Borneo. He'd like to go to Borneo one day, that'd be cool — or name a dance Borneo. Borneo, Borneo — it sounded like Romeo. Okay, that was it, it was way too hot. He unscrewed the cap on his water bottle and poured some into his mouth, but his cheeks were already rosy pink.

Mrs. Demidovski went up to the front of the room and started to talk quietly to Mr. Moretti, who started to frown.

Julian drank some more water and hiccupped. He began to stretch, the humidity made his body feel like elastic. It was great, as long as he didn't faint. "Why is it so hot in here?" he whispered to Tristan at the side of the room.

"I don't know," Tristan whispered back. "I think the thermostat or whatever controls the heating thingy might be broken."

"Taylor, Julian," Mr. Moretti said angrily. "Mrs. Demidovski wants me to see you two dance the *pas de deux* you have been rehearsing."

Julian gulped and looked at Taylor. She looked just as nervous on the outside as he felt. Around them everyone had turned to look at them, and the heat made them look annoyed and unforgiving.

"Quickly," Mr. Moretti snapped. "Show me."

Julian looked back at Taylor, and then he began to grin. He'd forgotten; this was a weird day, nothing that happened really mattered. He was too hot, too tired, and felt too strange to be nervous. "Come on, Tay," he said. "Let's do this."

Chapter Seven

Kaitlyn Wardle
You know you're cool when your iTunes most played
list has Tchaikovsky and Delibes at the top :p

Kaitlyn was not one of those people who liked to break
the rules. She believed that rules were there for a pur-
pose, and liked following them; it made her feel more
important than those who didn't. Sometimes, however,
she was forced to break the rules. Like yesterday, when
she had lied to some old dance friends. She stood in the
room of Social Studies students, giving a presentation on
Canadian pioneers that her mother had written for her,
and let her brain drift off to what had happened yesterday.

She had been talking to students from her old
school, and of course they had asked her if they could
watch her in *Coppelia*. She had told them that she didn't
know when it was yet, or anything really about it, which
was a lie; what she didn't know was if she was going to
be dancing Swanhilda or not. After everyone had found
out that Grace had probably not deserved to get the role,
she had thought that she would get it, but now she just
didn't know. Nobody did. Even Taylor had been dancing the role the other day — what was next, little Chloe
doing the role? Taylor probably wasn't going to do it, she

was still not that strong, but the point was that they had been considering her.

Her teacher asked her a question on one of the PowerPoint slides that she had been showing, and Kaitlyn stared at her blankly. "I don't know," she said.

She clicked the next slide; it had the answer. "Oh, it's here."

Her teacher looked unimpressed. "See me after class, Kaitlyn. Everyone, I would like to remind you that you should be doing your own work, not your tutor, not your parents, not whoever you could bribe to do it."

Kaitlyn blushed. "I *did* do it."

"Continue your presentation, Kaitlyn. We'll talk after class."

Kaitlyn was *so* unimpressed as she walked out of McKinley. Her teacher had zero proof, so all she had gotten was a pointless lecture, and now she was going to be late for class if she didn't hurry up. Why were adults so annoying sometimes? She walked up to the bus stop, and saw to her surprise that Alexandra was also waiting there. "Hey, Lexi," she said shyly. "How come you're late?"

Alexandra groaned. "Had to go see my counsellor. I have to do a couple of online courses in the summer, which is going to be so much fun to try and do while I'm at summer intensives."

"How come?"

"I'm missing some courses that I need to fulfil for Human Kinetics at UBC."

Kaitlyn stared at her, confused. "What? Why do you need to do that for? Aren't you going to be auditioning next year?"

"Yeah," Alexandra said. "But I still want to have everything ready in case. I think I want to do Human Kinetics if end up going to university, so I need to do these courses."

"Oh." Kaitlyn thought about that as they waited for the bus. She was going to be in grade ten next year, and Mr. Briggs had said that they were going to be planning their courses for next year soon. She had never thought about what she wanted to take in university. She didn't really like anything in school, and she'd never really thought about it; she was going to be a dancer, she didn't need to. The bus pulled up and they got on.

"How come you picked Human Kinetics?" she asked Alexandra, sitting carefully on the seat next to her.

Alexandra shrugged. "I don't know," she said. "I kind of like everything a lot, and Human Kinetics seems the most natural thing to do after dance — and if I aim for Human Kinetics and then I apply and don't get in, it's easier to get into arts." She opened up a small container of yogurt.

"Is that soy?" Kaitlyn asked, wrinkling her nose.

"Yes," Alexandra said, shrugging. "It's good — I've been thinking about trying to go vegan."

"I could never do that," Kaitlyn said feelingly.

Alexandra didn't bother to answer, and to Kaitlyn's embarrassment she put on her headphones and began reading *To Say Nothing of the Dog* instead of talking to

Kaitlyn. Kaitlyn began to eat her crackers and cheese. Her mother had finally decided that she could be in charge of her own lunch once she discovered that Kaitlyn was eating other stuff anyway.

Everyone else was already in the studio, so Kaitlyn hurried downstairs. Stupid teacher. At least she had contemporary with Sequoia for first class, so she didn't have to put her hair up. She changed into a bodysuit and tights, pulled a pair of black shorts over top, and ran up to the class. "Sorry I'm late," she said as she walked in.

"No problem," Sequoia said brightly. Sequoia had liked Kaitlyn a lot less ever since she hadn't shown up to YAGP. She had clearly been looking forward to the exposure that Kaitlyn's performance of her choreography would have given her. "We have just started working on a piece for June Show."

Kaitlyn stared at her, confused. "There are going to be two contemporary pieces in June Show?" she asked slowly. People had already been cast for the contemporary dance that the professional program students always did in the recreational students' end of year showcase.

"What do you mean *two*?" Sequoia asked sharply.

"Well, Leah is doing a small one — just a few people are in that one, though."

The room was very silent as everyone watched Sequoia process this information. It seemed to come as quite a shock to her, and she folded herself into a cross-legged position, stretched out her hands, and chanted,

"*Om, Hiranya varnam harinim/Suvarna rajatasrajam/ Chandraam hiranmayim/Lakshmim jatavedo ma avaha.*"

Her students watched her, not particularly surprised by her outburst. Sequoia's eyes suddenly popped open, and she redid her blond ponytail with firm hands. "Well. I didn't know that Leah was teaching at the academy now. I assumed that I would be the one to choreograph your contemporary piece, as I am your contemporary teacher — but I supposed that is too logical for the academy."

Her students watched her, warily. They had never seen her lose it before, and she looked dangerously close to it.

"I suppose they didn't feel the need to let me know that they weren't going to use my work," she continued.

Her lip trembled. Kaitlyn watched her, eyebrows raised.

"Nobody seems upset that I won't be choreographing your dance," Sequoia added in a tremulous voice.

Nobody dared to speak. None of them liked Sequoia's class: Tristan, Alexandra, and Anna hadn't even bothered to show up today. It was a standing — and not particularly funny — joke that she had the most boring class in the world.

"I do my best," Sequoia said, and then her face collapsed and she began to cry. "Why does everyone hate me? We should be supporting each other; I support you guys as artists, why don't you support me?"

Because you aren't any good, Kaitlyn answered her silently. She looked around; nobody seemed to know what to do.

"Should I go get Mrs. Demidovski?" Jessica asked. Nobody answered, and Jessica ran out of the room, appearing a few minutes later with that solver of all problems, Gabriel.

"Ah, ah, what is this?" he said uncomfortably. "Don't be upset in front of the children."

"Gabriel," Sequoia wailed, falling into Gabriel's arms. He held her awkwardly, fully cognizant of the legal issues involved with hugging attractive contemporary teachers. "Did you know, I'm not choreographing the contemporary dance for them, Leah is! She doesn't even teach at the academy."

"There, there," Gabriel reassured her, patting her awkwardly on the back. He appeared to think that acting English was the best way to handle the situation. "Do you want some tea?"

"Yes," Sequoia said, rubbing her wet nose. "Do you have any organic tea?"

"Hmm — yes," Gabriel lied quickly. "Come along to the office, I will make you some nice organic tea."

The students stared at each other as she left. "Well, that was my favourite class that she's taught all year," Keiko said dryly.

Kaitlyn giggled. "Me, too."

"Why did you get her to do your contemporary solo then?" Taylor asked quickly.

"Mr. Demidovski basically forced me into it. He wanted her to feel welcome. And I didn't realize how bad she was when I agreed."

They sat in silence for a moment, registering the

tragedy of being tricked into having Sequoia choreograph your solo.

Tristan popped his head in the door. "Hey, I just
saw Sequoia in the office, crying at poor Gabriel. What
happened?"

Kaitlyn shrugged. "She just found out that Leah
was choreographing the contemporary piece, and she
freaked out."

"Ha-ha, awesome." Tristan laughed. He still hadn't
forgiven Sequoia for telling him that he had to get in
touch with his masculine side during the first class she
had taught at the academy. "Get over here then. Anna's
here with everyone's Yumiko orders, and she won't let me
open the box until you guys are there." The room emp-
tied swiftly with everyone wanting to see their orders.

Kaitlyn walked more slowly after them. She hadn't
ordered anything this time. "Kaitlyn, look!" Taylor said,
spinning around. She was wearing a hot-pink halter
bodysuit with lime green edging, and Kaitlyn had to
blink to look at her. "Wow."

"Good wow or bad wow?"

"Good. You look like Barbie."

Taylor pouted. "I don't."

"You do."

"Old Barbie, or new one?"

"Uh, I didn't know that there were two."

Tristan was pirouetting in his new stretchy green
shirt with its orange stripes. Mr. Yu walked past them
and then backed up. "Not uniform," he said, frowning.

Tristan nodded. "Isn't it cool?"

"Hm," Mr. Yu said, his lip quivering with the effort of not laughing. "Cool? Okay, okay — you go change into uniform before class." He walked off.

"I hate uniform," Tristan sighed.

"I know." Kaitlyn's bodysuit had stretched out since September, and where it had been a nice dark colour, it was now faded. She'd had to knot up the straps to keep it from falling down her chest when she danced.

Tristan suddenly climbed up on the top of the table in the lunch room and held out his brightly coloured water bottle as if about to propose a toast. "As everyone knows," he began, "Anna has left the academy. It's very tragic." He paused, and everyone clapped automatically, Anna laughing. "Now," Tristan began again, "as Anna will probably not want to continue bringing us our Yumiko fixes, this leaves a very important post empty. I would like to nominate myself for that post. All in favour of me being the new Yumi-boy, raise your hand."

They all raised their hands, including Anna.

"All right then," Tristan said, keeping a straight face. "I propose to take over my duties in June. Thank you for your support everyone." He hopped off the table.

"Future politician in the making," Alexandra said sarcastically.

"I'd make an excellent politician." Tristan grinned, looking like a cross between Jim Carrey and a Disney kid. "Look at this smile. I'd have everyone's vote."

"Uh-huh," Alexandra said.

"I'd vote for you," Julian laughed. "You'd just have to do a few things for me first."

Tristan put his hands on his hips and stared at an imaginary list in the air. "Hm. Legalize marijuana. Done. Moon Stephen Harper. Double done."

"It's like you can read my mind," Julian laughed.

"Well, it's pretty easy." Tristan winked. "There's not much to it."

"Hey!"

Cromwell Gilly came around the corner and stopped, staring at them. His face lit up like someone had given him a new sewing machine. "Don't all of you have class?"

"Our teacher is currently in the middle of a nervous breakdown," Alexandra explained, swinging her legs as she sat on the counter of the academy's mini dance-supply store. "We have ballet in half an hour, though."

"Boys," Cromwell Gilly said immediately, "go down and get the blue trunks on the left of the costume room door. We can get your costumes sorted out now."

Tristan, Kageki, Jonathon, and Julian went down-stairs to grab the trunks.

Cromwell Gilly flung open the doors of the large studio and proceeded to attempt to sort them. "People who are just dancing Villagers, here. Who is dancing flower *pas*? Who is Swanhilda?"

There was a very dramatic silence. "Doesn't anyone know what they are dancing?" Cromwell Gilly asked, exasperated.

"Well, no," Alexandra said quietly, "we don't really. It's a bit of a long story."

"I hate the Demidovskis," Cromwell Gilly moaned. He sank to the floor, sitting there as he thought, tapping his exceptionally lovely leather shoes on the floor. The boys came up with the trunks. "Set them over on the side," Cromwell Gilly said. "All right, here is what is going to happen: everyone who might possibly be playing Swanhilda, stand on the side, everyone else go pick a costume and only share it with someone who is dancing a different cast than you." Cromwell Gilly waited patiently for them to do as he asked. To his surprise Alexandra, Kaitlyn, Grace, Taylor, and Aiko all were waiting at the side. He frowned. "You can't all be potentially Swanhilda?" he exclaimed. "That's five of you, and the show is in, what, a month?"

Alexandra shrugged. "It's really just me and Aiko," she said quickly, stepping forward before anyone could protest. "We can try on the costumes if you want, and the rest can try the Friends costumes."

Cromwell Gilly eyed her, knowing exactly how full of rot she was. But he liked Alexandra, so he replied, "All right then. I just hope no one comes crying to me when they're missing a costume. That's a sob story that you'll have to take directly to the Demidovskis." With that he swigged some water like it was the something stronger that he wished he had, and got to work. "Children! Order. These are the Villagers costumes, these are the Friends ..."

Grace left the room. Kaitlyn didn't know what to do. Should she disobey Alexandra and try to get a costume? No, she did not want to risk Alexandra's wrath. She turned and followed Grace out of the door, down to the change rooms. She found Grace crying at her lockers. "What's wrong?" Kaitlyn asked awkwardly. She was never very good with other people's emotions; they always seemed to get upset about things that she didn't care about.

"Like you don't know," Grace snapped. "This whole stupid school has been gossiping about it for weeks. I am *this* close to following Anna to a different school."

"That would be stupid," Kaitlyn said bluntly. "Then you'll never be a ballet dancer. I think you should just suck it up."

Grace raised her rather red face and glared at her. "Who asked you? You should go eat something so your butt can get a little bigger."

Kaitlyn was at a loss for words. She could take jokes about her weight from Taylor, or from Alexandra, but from Grace? Grace was practically at normal weight herself. She did the only thing that she could; she turned around and walked off. The clock said that it was almost time for ballet class.

Upstairs, Mr. Yu was trying to kick Cromwell Gilly out of the studio so that he could teach, but Cromwell Gilly just kept flitting out of his reach, ignoring him as he tried to organize everyone's costumes. Finally Mr. Yu had had enough. He reached out and picked Cromwell Gilly up, carrying him easily out of the studio and setting him in the hall. "I said out!"

Cromwell Gilly sighed. "Fine. But I won't be doing any last-minute fittings this year. Do you hear me?" he called as Mr. Yu disappeared into the studio, closing the door behind him. "I won't!"

Mr. Yu walked to the centre of the classroom. "Boys, take trunks to side," he commanded, annoyed. "This is class time, not costume time. Girls, take costume off." He turned to the piano to tell George what to play, but to his confusion there was no George. He looked around like the pianist might suddenly emerge from the walls. "Where is George? Go look outside, see if he is smoking," Mr. Yu said to Kaitlyn. She nodded and went to the side door of the building. There was a small alleyway full of old metal staircases and garbage bins where most of the academy instructors went to smoke. The wind made her cold as she opened the door in her uniform. There was no George. She looked down the street to the north — there was an old homeless man walking by eating a hamburger. She looked south — there was George, pedalling fast on his old rickety bike. If George had been thirty years younger he would have made the perfect hipster, with his pianist hands, collection of plaid shirts, and old jeans that always seemed to have the left leg rolled up to show a thick woollen sock.

"George," she said as he parked his bike at the side of the building, "Mr. Yu wants you."

George snorted. He dug a cigarette out of his sock and lit it, his hands purple from holding the handlebars in the wind. In the enclosed alleyway it was calmer, but outside the branches kept whipping and Kaitlyn saw a branch lying on the sidewalk. "He does, does he? He wants me. Well, it's nice to be needed." As he smoked, Kaitlyn watched him, worried. In a school full of dramatic, overemotional people, George was the calm one, the one who had seen everything and let nothing faze him.

"What's wrong, George?"

George shook his head, sitting down on the metal steps beside where he stood. Kaitlyn crouched beside him, not wanting to sit in her body suit on the dirty steps. "Young people don't want to hear the troubles of the old," he said bitterly.

Kaitlyn shook her head. "I want to hear," she protested. George wavered. "Tell me, George, please?"

"All right. It's not that interesting. There was a man — let's call him Dick."

"Dick. Got it."

"Yeah. Now, Dick, he was really good at playing the piano — not brilliant, but good. When he was a kid his parents were proud of him for that, you know? And then when he got older he learned how to play the guitar, because girls think guitarists are sexier, but he always loved something about the piano." George smoked, and Kaitlyn was silent. "This guy, he thought that maybe he would become a great pianist, one of those guys that has their own CD and everyone dresses up to go and see, right? Or maybe he would play the piano in a famous rock and roll band."

Kaitlyn waited, but that seemed to be the end of the story. "What happened next?"

"Well, then his girlfriend got pregnant, and he had to get a job, and he started playing the piano for dance classes around the city. He was good at that, all the schools wanted him, and soon he was mostly playing for one good school that paid him well, and guesting around at others. Dick liked that, because he could see all the young dancers growing up and following their dreams. Then he turned fifty, and that kid he had? He's grown up, and he plays the guitar, and he wants to make a living off of that."

"Isn't that good?" Kaitlyn asked. "Your son is probably really good at playing the guitar, like you're really good at the piano."

George smiled as he thought about that. "Yeah. He's really good. I just want something better for him."

"You want him to make more money."

George was silent for a moment. "I guess it does all come down to that, doesn't it?" He sighed. "I feel old. And I don't like it. Anybody who tells you they like getting old? Don't believe a word of it. Sure, there are good things about getting old — maturity, better taste in wine — but Dylan Thomas had it right, Kaitlyn. *Do not go gentle into that good night, Old age should burn and rave at close of day.*" He put his hand on her shoulder. "Come on, I'd better go in before Yu is forced to do his raging tiger imitation."

Chapter Eight

Taylor woke up early, trying to remember why on earth her
alarm would be set for such a hideous time of day. *Oh.* She
had auditions today. She sat up, accidentally kicking Keiko.
She'd forgotten that Keiko was sleeping over. She hopped
out of bed and put her yellow bunny slippers on, walking
to the kitchen. Charlize was already in the kitchen. "Good,
you're up. I was just going to go get you — where's Keiko?"

"She's still asleep." Taylor dug in the fridge for some
chocolate milk and began to sip it. "Mom, can you
make pancakes?"

"Taylor, we have to leave in an hour."

"So?"

"Okay, I'll make pancakes if you are completely
ready, everything in the car, hair done, by the time that
they are made."

"Thanks. I'll go wake up Keiko." Taylor padded
along back to her room. "Keiko! Keiko, Keiko, Keiko —"
Keiko merely turned over. Taylor considered the situation. She reached out and took one of Keiko's hairs and
stuck it in her nostril, tickling it.

"Ah!" Keiko sat up, annoyed. She rubbed her nose. "What are you doing, Taylor?"

Taylor jumped up on her bed. "You wouldn't get up. My dad used to do that to me when I was little."

"Your dad is a crazy man." Keiko grabbed a pillow and buried her face in it. "Agh, agh, agh." She finally got up and went over to her bag of toiletries, digging out a small box of pills. She took two and swallowed.

"What are those for?" Taylor asked.

Keiko frowned at her. "Just medicine."

"For what?"

"My people allergy."

"What do you mean your people allergy?"

"Don't you know that it is rude to ask people about pills? It is for my people allergy."

"Um, okay? My mom says that she will make us pancakes if we get completely ready really fast."

"Okay." Keiko went into the bathroom and started to brush her teeth. Taylor followed her, and began to do her hair. She took some parts of her ponytail out to twist and make coiled lines on top of the smooth regular ponytail.

"Keiko, what is a people allergy?"

Keiko looked at her. "It is something I take a pill for. The pill makes me calm, and then I don't hate people."

"Oh." Taylor considered this. "I don't think we have people allergies in Canada. It must be just a thing that is in Japan."

Keiko ignored this and began doing her makeup. She did the best eyes of anybody in the school, by the end whichever eyes she had been working on looked 50 percent larger.

Taylor watched her. "Can you do my eyes, Keiko?"

"No."

"Why?"

"Because I want pancakes." This was a valid reason, so Taylor turned around to the mirror and started to work.

"You girls ready?" Charlize called up to them.

"Coming." They went downstairs with their large overflowing bags.

"I am sure that you guys don't actually need that much stuff," Charlize protested. Alison was already sitting at the table, and there was a large stack of pancakes in the centre of the table.

"Yes, we do," Taylor said firmly. "I haven't decided which bodysuits and which *pointe* shoes I am going to wear yet." She took the fork and pulled three pancakes off of the plate, organizing them in a triangular shape so that the maximum surface area was available for butter and maple syrup.

Keiko eyed Taylor's plate disgustedly and then pulled three pancakes out for herself, stacking them precisely on top of each other and pouring a small amount of maple syrup onto the side of her plate so that she could dip bits of the pancakes in it. Beside Taylor, Alison was too busy playing games on Charlize's iPhone to eat. Charlize watched her youngest daughter. "Alison, eat."

"I'm not hungry." Alison met Charlize's eyes with a firm stare. If Taylor was easy for Charlize to manipulate, Alison was the stubborn opposite.

"That's what you said at dinner last night."

"It's the truth." Alison shrugged.

Taylor looked at her, slightly confused. She was pretty sure she had not been this annoying when she had been eight. "Alison, eat it. It's, like, really good. There are chocolate chips in it."

"I don't want to."

"Fine." Charlize took Alison's plate away, giving up. Alison got up and left the table, going into the living room to watch TV.

"I don't know what's wrong with her," Taylor whispered to Keiko. "She keeps doing that."

Keiko stared at her. "Are you stupid? She's dieting."

Taylor frowned. "No. She's eight."

Keiko shook her head. "But her tummy is maybe same size as yours. She doesn't look like you and your mother."

"Yeah, she looks like Dad. So?"

"Maybe she doesn't like that." Keiko finally finished her breakfast and took it to the sink, washing it and putting it on the drying rack. Taylor dumped hers in the sink. They went and got their coats, and everyone got into the car.

"Oh, guys," Charlize said as she pulled out of the driveway, "your dad is going to meet us for dinner in Seattle after the audition, all right?"

"Yay!" Taylor shrieked. She hadn't seen her dad since he had come to see her *Nutcracker* performance, and she had really missed him. He wasn't very good at talking on the phone, so she hadn't talked to him much, either; they'd had one conversation when Charlize had angrily forced him to call her after she dropped out of school, but that was it.

"Are we going to pick up Julian?" Alison asked hopefully. Julian was her favourite of Taylor's friends, a fact that she had no problem repeating incessantly.

"No, Julian is getting a ride with Tristan." They continued on to Seattle, Taylor curling up into a ball and trying to fall asleep using her Lululemon hoodie as a pillow.

As they pushed open the doors of Pacific Northwest Ballet's studios, Charlize groaned. There was a long line-up to sign in at the audition. "I'll wait, you guys go get changed," she said.

Keiko and Taylor ran to the back, knowing where the bathrooms were from previous auditions. Taylor changed into a nice purple bodysuit, Keiko into a black one. Taylor frowned, looking at the two of them in the mirror. "Don't you want to wear something that will make you stand out more?"

"No," Keiko said firmly. "Black looks nice and professional."

"Okay ..." Taylor's phone went off, and she checked it. She had a text from Julian.

> Are you there yet?
>
> Yup. U?
>
> No. There was drama. Tell you about in a few — can u try to get our numbers/sign us in?
>
> Kk, see ya.

Taylor turned to Keiko. "I have to go tell Mom to get Julian and Tristan's numbers, something's wrong, they might be late."

"Okay. I'm going to go stretch in the hallway."

Taylor ran out of the bathroom and to the front of the line where Charlize was about to sign them in. "Can you get Julian and Tristan's stuff too?" she asked. "They're going to be late."

"Okay." Charlize shrugged. "Go stretch please, okay, Taylor?"

"Fine! I was just about to go do it. You don't have to tell me to do everything, you know." Taylor went grumpily off and found Keiko, who had found Kaitlyn. "Oh, hey ... I didn't know that you were auditioning for American Ballet Theatre."

"I didn't know you didn't know." Kaitlyn shrugged. "We're even." She began to stretch feet with Keiko.

"Which location do you want to go to?" Taylor asked, curious.

"I haven't decided," Kaitlyn lied. Before Taylor could question her further, they were interrupted by Alexandra coming to sit down beside them.

"You're auditioning, too?" Taylor asked.

Alexandra shrugged. "Why not? It's good to have a backup summer intensive."

Taylor gulped. ABT was definitely not her "backup" summer intensive, she really wanted to go.

"Look, there are Julian and Tristan!" Keiko said, pointing through the dancers sprawled on the floor. Tristan and Julian were getting their numbers and forms from Charlize. They made their way over to the girls. Julian had a huge dopey grin on his face, and Tristan looked like he was about to skip.

"What?" Taylor said impatiently. "Come on, what happened? Why were you late?"

"So," Tristan said slowly, sitting down in a chair beside them and looking down on them. "We — me and Julian — decided to go take class before we came here, with the Youth Company."

"Can Julian tell this story?" Alexandra said impatiently. "He speaks faster than you."

Tristan glared at her. "Do you want to hear what happened, or not?"

"Kk, so," Julian said quickly. "We were taking class, and then Aiko comes in — she's a little bit late, which Aiko never is, right? So Mr. Moretti asked 'Why are you late?' and she said 'I had to talk to the Demidovskis,' and he was like 'Why? Or is it personal?' and she said, 'No, I have to tell you too — I cannot dance Swanhilda, because I got a job with Het Nationale Ballet,' and Mr. Moretti, he was in shock, I think? He was very confused, he just stood there, and then he was like, 'You can't dance Swanhilda? My congratulations, of course, but you can't dance Swanhilda?' and then she was just like '... no.'" Julian took a deep breath.

"And that is why Julian should never be allowed to tell stories," Tristan said bitterly. "But, that is just the first half."

"Wait, slow down," Alexandra stopped him. "So, Aiko is moving to Holland before she can dance Swanhilda?"

"Yes."

"Okay, go on ..."

"And then Leon said that he was going with her, to dance in a very small contemporary company, and everyone was like 'Whaaaaaaat?' Inception, mind blown, Leon isn't going to be here? So he's leaving, too."

"There's going to be no one left soon," Kaitlyn said sadly.

"This happens every year," Tristan said impatiently. "You just don't know because you only came last September. But then, then, guess who showed up to audition?"

"Me?" Nat said dryly from behind them. Tristan screamed and fell out of his chair. Around them, other dancers shot them dirty looks. Nat wasn't dressed in dance clothes; he was in his normal street clothes. Taylor had seen him dance at YAGP, but she'd never met him in real life. He was much better-looking in his street clothes.

"Er, hi, Nat," Tristan said, embarrassed. "What's up?"

"I thought your sister said that you were going to Royal Ballet School in the fall?" Alexandra said accusingly.

"Yes," Nat agreed. "But the parentals are making a fuss lately — they don't think that I am mature enough to survive all by my wee infant self in England. They wanted me to audition for the Vancouver ... Vancouver ..."

"Vancouver International Ballet Academy," Tristan supplied helpfully.

"Yes, that. Why ever did they name it such an atrocious thing?"

"Vanity," Alexandra answered. "You can just call it the academy. That's what we do."

"How very ethnocentric of you," Nat retorted. "*The* academy? The only one? Anyway, my lovely parents are moving to Vancouver for a year starting in September, and they would really be over the moon if I went to your charming school."

"But you don't want to," Tristan finished for him.

"Not remotely," Nat said apologetically. "Lux might join you, though. I think she has some idea that it might have good training. An opinion that she got from watching you dance," he added, nodding at Alexandra.

Alexandra blushed. "Um, thanks."

"Can everyone please line up?" a lady by the sign-in desk called out.

"Oh, crap!" Taylor exclaimed. She had been so busy watching the skit playing out in front of her that she hadn't even put her number on yet. She hastily attached it to her bodysuit, and then they went into the huge studio, leaving Nat behind. As she walked in, a sudden thought occurred to her: *Why is Nat here if he's not auditioning?*

Taylor was exhausted by the time she got out of the studio, but Charlize pounced immediately. "How did it go?"

"Good, I think," Taylor said, shrugging. "I messed up an exercise, but my jumps were really good."

"Okay. You and Keiko go get changed and meet us in the front. Your audition went longer than it was supposed to. We're going to be late to meet your father."

"Oh crap. Okay." Taylor ran to the bathroom to get changed, Keiko hurrying after her.

"What is the rush?" Keiko asked. "He is your dad, he will wait."

"Yeah," Taylor said. "But what if he doesn't? I really want to see him, Keiko. Come on." Taylor pulled out her bun, leaving her long blond hair in a ponytail curling down her back. There wasn't enough time to take her hair all the way down without it looking gross. They walked down to the end of the lobby, passing the others who were still talking. "Bye, guys." Taylor froze, and then ran back. "Hey," she said, addressing Nat, "how come you came here if you aren't auditioning?"

Nat grinned. "Lux," he explained.

"I didn't see her in the audition, either."

"You must have missed her. It was a big audition."

Taylor frowned. She was confused; she'd been looking for Lux, and she was almost positive that she had not seen her. Still, Nat was right, it had been a big audition and she could have missed her. "Oh. Well, see ya."

"See ya around, child."

Taylor ran to catch up with Keiko, still a little confused. "Come on," Keiko said. "Your mother is going crazy; she wants to know why you won't hurry up." Keiko pointed across the street where Charlize was standing, waving at them to come over. They hurried across the street and got into the car.

"Now, let's see if I can find this place," Charlize said, handing Taylor a sheet of paper with the address on it. "Can you get the GPS to work, Taylor?"

"Sure."

It had started to rain, hard, and the wind was whipping around. It was not typical May weather. "You'd think we were in Vancouver, it's raining so much," Taylor said, peering out the window. She wouldn't have admitted it to Keiko, who would have laughed at her, but the weather scared her. It reminded her of old horror films she had watched in grade seven. Horror films had been popular when she was twelve; the best way to show you were the coolest was to let nothing scare you. Taylor had always been fine while she was watching the movie, but afterwards she'd get nightmares.

"April showers bring May flowers," Charlize said brightly. "I think Mother Nature must have reversed it! April was sunny, now May is stormy."

"Oh geez, Mom," Taylor said, disgusted as Charlize started laughing hysterically at her own joke. A branch fell down with a crash beside the road, and Charlize screamed, nearly veering onto the side of the road. "*Mom!*"

To Taylor's surprise, instead of continuing on, her mother pulled to the side of the road. "Mom, it was only a branch."

Charlize turned off the car and rested her forehead on the steering wheel for a moment.

"Mom?"

Charlize took a deep breath. "I'm all right. It just scared me, that's all."

"Oh."

Charlize pulled back onto the road, and they started on their way again, following the directions of the GPS lady. "How come Daddy is here?" Taylor asked, for the sake of something to say.

"You should ask him that," Charlize said briefly. "There, is that it, girls?"

"I think so," Keiko answered. "Yes."

They got out of the car. Taylor pulled her hood up over her hair — the rain and wind were so strong that they were going to ruin her hair in the thirty-second walk to the restaurant. They walked in, and Charlize shoved Taylor in front of her. "Can you see your father?" she asked.

Taylor looked around. "There he is. We're just going to join my dad, he's over there," she told the hostess who was hurrying up to them. They walked down to him, and Taylor saw that he was not alone. "Oh, hi …"

"Oh hi to you, too, princess." Steven laughed. "Hi, Charlize. Alison, you're getting bigger every time I see you. And who's this?"

"Keiko. You met her before, remember?"

"Oh, of course I did! Sorry, I forgot."

They all sat down, Taylor finding herself across from her father and beside her mother. Alison had slipped beside her dad. "So, um —" Taylor asked pointedly. There was a woman next to her father, and Taylor knew who she was, but she wanted an introduction.

"Oh! This is Vivienne, everyone. Vivienne, my ex-wife, Charlize, and our two beautiful daughters, and of course, Keiko."

"Isn't this cozy," Charlize muttered, so quietly that only Taylor could hear. Taylor giggled. She stared at

Vivienne, slightly confused. She wasn't sure why, but she had assumed that Vivienne would look like her mother, but she didn't, not at all. Vivienne was Korean, and short, and wearing dark clothing. Taylor thought that her mother looked a million times prettier.

"So what have you been up to, sweetheart?" Steven asked, staring at Taylor.

"Um, I've been dancing a lot. I might be playing Swanhilda in the June production of *Coppelia*. Swanhilda's, like, the lead. And I got an agent, I'm doing some acting stuff. I auditioned for *Superbly Unnatural* last week, but for a dancing role, not an acting role."

"Good, good … sounds like you're doing well. How's your boy, the one I met the last time I saw you?"

"Julian? Daddy, he's not my boy. And I think he might be gay."

"Oh. Good, good … you can do better, anyway. Wasn't he a hippie?" He looked down at his menu. "Everyone decided what they want to order yet?"

"Aren't you forgetting something?" Charlize asked pointedly.

"What?" Steven asked impatiently. "Look, if you want more time to order, Charlize, just let me know, don't play games."

Charlize's eyes flashed, and Taylor tensed. It was never a good sign when Charlize got mad. "You have two daughters, *Steven*."

Steven looked to his left. "Ah. How are you, Alison?"

"Good."

"See? She's good. Now, can we please order? I'm starving."

Taylor was unusually quiet as they drove home. It was late, but the wind was calmer. Alison and Keiko had both fallen asleep, and Taylor had tried, but she couldn't. "Mom?"

"Yes, baby?"

"Does Daddy not like Alison?"

"Of course he loves Ali!" Charlize said quickly, looking back to make sure that Alison was asleep.

"Does he like me better, though?"

Charlize was quiet, thinking. "You are just easier for him, Taylor," she said. "He finds it easier to relate to you."

"Well, it's not fair! Alison didn't do anything."

"Taylor, I don't feel like talking about this right now. Go to sleep."

"Mom?"

"What, Taylor?"

"Daddy asked me if I wanted to go and live with him and Vivienne next fall." Taylor could hear her mother stop breathing. "I told him no. I didn't want to stop going to the academy. He wanted me to focus on acting and stuff in L.A."

Charlize started breathing again. "You said no because you wanted to keep going to the academy."

"Yeah."

"Go to sleep, Taylor." Taylor bent her head down and closed her eyes, wondering if she had made the right decision. The real reason she had said no to Steven had been that she could not picture living with him. He had never really been home when she was younger, and she couldn't remember ever having a full conversation with him. And Vivienne — she didn't like Vivienne. Vivienne didn't give off any vibes of what she was like, and Taylor liked people that let you know who they were right away. *Like Julian.* Taylor buried her face in her sweatshirt, turning her face to the window so Charlize couldn't see her face. She'd managed to forget that she liked Julian, but her dad bringing him up had made her remember that she liked him all over again. That was why she had told Zack that she wasn't sure that she wanted to go out with him. Maybe she would tell Julian that Zack had asked her out, and see how he reacted.

Chapter Nine

Alexandra Dunstan
My feet have reached a new level of grossness. I have a
blister on top of a blister on top of a blister.

Alexandra crawled out from under the large prop wagon
that was full of fake flowers, triumphantly dangling her
canvas shoe in front of her. "Hah!" she said aloud. She
kept losing her canvas shoes, and she knew someone was
taking and hiding them. She had her suspicions that it
was Jessica; it seemed exactly the sort of weird and neu-
rotic thing she would do. She put the shoe on and stood
up, wiggling her foot around until it was in perfectly.

"How'd you lose your shoe under there?" Julian
asked, laughing.

Alexandra looked out, shading her eyes against the
stage lights as she tried to see into the audience. "Julian?"
She walked to the edge of the stage, where she could see
him. "Hey. It depends on what you mean by losing."

"Er, how else would you explain a situation where
you are climbing hilariously out from under a wagon
looking extremely pleased with yourself?"

Alexandra jumped off of the stage and walked over
to him. "Three words. Some. Bitch. Stole."

"Oh."

"Yes." Alexandra sat down next to him. "What is new in the wonderful world of Julian?"

"Nothing much. Who's stealing your shoes?"

"I'm guessing Jessica, but I'm basing that on absolutely nothing but the fact that I hate her."

"Hate is a strong word. It is virtually impossible to hate something without also loving it."

"Not true. Okay, I strongly dislike her. Don't distract me, I had something to ask you —" Alexandra thought for a moment. "Oh. I remember — what is it that you thought I was going to ask you about? That time that you were at my house?"

Julian frowned. "Nothing."

Alexandra stopped, staring at him. "Now I know it isn't nothing. Come on, tell me."

"No."

"How come?"

"Because. We aren't exactly friends, and I don't trust you to not tell everyone you find."

"I can keep a secret!"

"What about when Anna was quitting?"

"Okay, that was different, that was Anna."

"What about when you told me that Tristan liked me?"

"I thought you already knew that."

"My point is, no. I don't need to tell you, and I'm not going to."

"Uh, okay." Alexandra looked away, confused, annoyed, and hurt in almost equal measures. She didn't know why it was that she cared what Julian thought about her, but apparently she did. And the more she thought about it, the more pissed off she got. "I'm going to go check if we are likely to start this rehearsal any time in the next century."

She walked up the stage steps and through the wings to the backstage area. Mr. Yu was still looking at some sheets of paper and arguing with Mr. Demidovski. They were clearly going to be a while. Alexandra kept going, not sure in which direction she was walking, until she hit the change rooms. She turned around and walked back to the stage, not wanting to deal with the noise of the change rooms, and looped back to the audience, taking the door entry into the audience this time instead of cutting across the stage. Julian was still sitting in the front, but she ignored him, lying on the rich red carpet of the audience floor. It was probably filthy, but it was comforting. She looked upwards, at the ceiling so high above her. *I wonder how much of my life I will spend in theatres when I am dancing with a company. I hope I get a job with a company that travels a lot, and is in Europe. That would be so sweet. Or somewhere like San Francisco, or maybe New York.*

"You asleep down there?"

Julian was looking down at her, leaning over the back of one of the seats. "I'm not talking to you, Jules." She closed her eyes again, firmly.

She could hear Julian laugh above her. "Why, because I called you out for being a blabbermouth?"

"Yes."

"I didn't mean to hurt your feelings. I mean, there's nothing wrong with being a blabbermouth."

"Tell me something. If you won't tell me what I want to know, tell me a different secret. Then I'll keep that one, and you will see that I can."

Alexandra kept her eyes shut as she waited for him to pick.

"So many secrets, I don't know which one," Julian joked.

"An interesting one."

"Hm. Well, how about I just tell you a story, and you have to not tell anyone, okay?"

"All right."

"Okay. So my parents, they were at this music festival, right? And they'd broken up, but they were still friends. This would've been about August, there's sun shining down everywhere. At least, that's what my dad's friend told me. He was there, too."

"Sun. Got it."

"Yes. Anyway, they were all listening to the music, having a great time, and then suddenly my mom, she leans over to my dad and she's like, 'Will, I'm pregnant. We're going to have a kid.'"

"Did he freak out?"

"No. He stared at her, and he's a bit confused, because of the sun, and what she said, and stuff, so he's looking at her to see if she's joking. But she's not. So he says the first thing that pops into his head, which is, 'what are we going to name it?'"

"That is *not* what I would have asked."

"Shush. So, my mom, she doesn't know. She hadn't even thought about it. So, my dad goes 'Well, if it's a boy, let's name him Julian.' My mom, she says, 'What?

145

Like John Lennon's kid?' And Will, he says, 'Yes.' And my mom, she's like, 'Well, what if it's a girl?' and Will, he's like, 'We could name her Julian, too.'"

Alexandra giggled. "Good thing you are a boy, huh?"

"Yup." Julian smiled down at her.

"How will you know if I told anyone or not?"

"I have my ways." There was a commotion behind them. They both turned around, staring at the stage as everyone flooded it. "Better get up there."

"*Si.*" Alexandra stood up, and they walked over to the stage. Mr. Demidovski and Mr. Moretti were already up there, and the dancers arranged themselves behind them, sitting on the stage. Mr. Yu stood off to one side, watching the goings-on with an expression of wariness.

"As you all know," Mr. Demidovski begun, resting his hand over his heart, "we have had much, much trouble deciding who is to play the role of Swanhilda."

The dancers nodded their agreement. Seated beside Julian, Alexandra felt her stomach lurch. She sat up straighter. *Please, please, please …*

"We have decided —"

"Hello everyone!" Theresa beamed at them, walking into the audience with a swirl of scarves. "Oops! Am I interrupting something?"

Mr. Moretti nodded, annoyed.

"Sorry." Theresa sat down in the audience, quite ruining the setup, as now Mr. Demidovski was delivering a speech to his students in the front and Theresa was watching in the back. Mr. Demidovski had not been trained in the art of performing in a circus ring, and he lost his flow for a second.

"There has been much difficulty," Mr. Demidovski said. Alexandra groaned inwardly. He'd been about to get to it, but now there was no stopping the long speech. "Aiko has left. To Europe. We, of course, are very happy for her." Mr. Demidovski's dour expression contradicted the positive sentiments that he was expressing. "Anna — we very much loved Anna, but she has left." Mr. Demidovski bowed his head, as if in prayer or remembrance.

"By the way, how's that going with your brother and her?" Julian whispered.

"Shush," Alexandra hissed, paying attention to Mr. Demidovski.

"Grace ..." Mr. Demidovski looked thoughtful. "Yes. And then of course, Alexandra and Taylor."

Come on, please just say it ... but not if I didn't get it.

"So, first cast we have Alexandra. Second cast, Grace. Understudy, Taylor." Alexandra let her breath out. *Thank you, thank you ... wait, Taylor? They're actually giving it to Taylor?*

Suddenly somebody stood up and ran backstage. Alexandra stared after her. "Was that Kaitlyn?"

"Yeah." Julian stood up. "Want me to go check on her?" he asked Mr. Demidovski.

"Sit down," Mr. Moretti said impatiently.

Julian sat. "Damn it," he whispered to Alexandra. "I need to move, sitting here is driving me crazy."

"You'll survive," Alexandra said dryly.

"And of course, Liam has left," Mr. Demidovski continued.

"Leon," Mr. Moretti corrected.

"Ley-an. Yes. He has gone, and will not dance the part of Frantz."

Julian sat up straighter. "Want to talk about my brother's love life now?" Alexandra whispered. Julian pinched her, keeping his eyes focused on Mr. Demidovski. "Ow!"

Mr. Demidovski looked out at them. "First cast should be Dimitri. Second, should be Tristan. Understudy, should be Jonathon. Sorry to Kageki, you are too short." Mr. Demidovski did look genuinely sorry when he said that — Kageki was far too short to partner any of the girls that Mr. Demidovski had listed.

Mr. Moretti looked mad. He bent down and whispered into Mr. Demidovski's ear, but Alexandra was too far away to hear what they were saying. Beside her, Julian was slumped, looking at the floor. "Julian," Alexandra whispered.

"What?" Julian sounded as if he was trying very hard to sound normal, but his voice came out squeaky.

"Look up." Julian raised his head from his knees. Mr. Moretti was still arguing with Mr. Demidovski. "What — or who — do you think that they are most likely to be arguing about?"

Julian's face lit up, and then fell again. "Mr. Moretti doesn't even like me," he protested.

"I think he might," Alexandra argued.

"Okay, okay, Mr. Demidovski has to go. Please have a good dress rehearsal. Mr. Yu!" Mr. Demidovski waved his hand and Mr. Yu suddenly came alive again. "Come on, come on, everybody to places for first act, we rehearse first cast," he shouted, driving Mr. Moretti off the stage by sheer volume and energy. "Come on, come on!"

Julian sprang to his feet and reached out his hand to pull Alexandra up.

"Julian!" Taylor said, running over. "Did you see, did you see? I got understudy! Omigod, I am so happy!"

"Yeah. Congratulations." Julian's voice was strangely flat, but Taylor didn't seem to notice, hugging him anyway. Alexandra watched the two of them, frowning slightly. Their friendship got on her nerves. She couldn't say why, but she didn't like it; it annoyed her.

Grace came up, smiling, and gave Alexandra a hug. "Swanhilda buddies!"

"Yeah!"

Alexandra smiled. It was kind of nice to have Anna out of the picture, and now that they had both been cast as Swanhilda, maybe they could go back to being friends again. "Do you want to run through it once with me while Mr. Yu is rehearsing Villagers?"

"I would totally love to help you learn the steps," Grace assured her, "but I have to go find my mom, she said she was going to be bringing my lunch."

Alexandra stared after her, and made a face.

Tristan came up behind her. "Did you just stick your tongue out at Grace?"

"Yes, Tris, I asked her if she wanted to rehearse with me, and she twisted it around so it was like I was asking her to teach it to me."

"Oh. Kk, you have to come and help, though, Mr. Yu wants us to move the curtains over here before the camera crew comes."

"What camera crew?"

"Mr. Demidovski invited media people to watch us."

"But we're not remotely ready!"

"I don't think that occurred to Mr. Demidovski. Don't worry, everything will be fine. If anything goes wrong, just smile, they won't notice anything."

"Ready, light on. Left," Mr. Yu said into his headpiece, his accent sounding stronger through the crackles on the mike. Alexandra had the greatest sympathy for the backstage crew; she was not entirely sure how they managed to interpret his commands. Her theory was that they probably just guessed.

Mr. Yu turned to Alexandra. "Ready?" he asked.

Alexandra nodded, smiling.

"Good." Mr. Yu hugged her with one arm. "Be good." Alexandra nodded again, and went to the wing that she was supposed to come out of. There was a reason that Mr. Yu was one of her favourite teachers. He might act like a six-year-old, but he also felt like one of them. He was basically the antithesis of Mr. Moretti's cold removal. Alexandra waited in the wings, testing out her feet. The tendons felt warm, loose, and flexible. She breathed in, expanding her chest against the tight bodice of her costume, and letting the air out again. She really loved this kind of costume. It reminded her of the Cinderella costume she'd worn for Halloween when she was four, and five, and six — when she was seven her mother had told her that she had lost it, but now that she was sixteen, Alexandra had her suspicions. Her foot felt *really* loose. She wiggled it around a bit, and was rewarded with a sharp stabbing pain. *Agh.* She just had to suck it up for this run-through, and then she would go home and ice it.

Alexandra limped on her way out of the studio. She could feel her foot getting cold and tightening — it was going to hurt in the morning. Her cellphone went off, and she picked it up — it was Leah. "Hey …"

"Hey! Lexi, so glad I got ahold of you, I've been trying for the last two hours."

"Sorry, I've been in rehearsal. We're down at the Centre doing dress rehearsal for *Coppelia*."

"Okay, okay … wait, so you're downtown?"

"Yeah."

"Go to the front of the theatre, I'll pick you up."

"Wait, what?"

"See you in five."

Alexandra hung up on Leah, her favourite contemporary teacher. She had no idea what Leah could want, but whatever it was it was probably very interesting. She limped out to the front of the theatre and sat down on one of the large sand-coloured blocks of cement, watching for Leah's car. *There it is.* Leah's car was unmistakable, a low-slung, bright-red affair with stickers all over the back. Leah was fond of saying that understatement was for those who were afraid, and that philosophy apparently applied to her car, as well. Alexandra walked, or limped, out to the car and got in the front seat.

"What the hell is wrong with you?" Leah demanded.

Alexandra shrugged. "It's my ankle — it really hurts, I pulled or twisted something, I think."

"But you got through dress rehearsal no problem, right?"

"Yeah — sort of — it hurts a lot more now that I'm cold."

"Glove compartment. There's got to be some Tylenol in there."

Alexandra obediently began to dig around in the glove compartment, pulling out no fewer than six bottles of Tylenol, two of Advil, a couple packets of prescription painkillers, and a large bottle of Aleve.

"You plan on being in a lot of pain during the zombie apocalypse?" Alexandra asked dryly.

"Shut up and take some Tylenol. Put those bottles back," Leah said testily. "Okay, so we're going to Harbour — they're casting some new pilot or whatever, anyway, they're having an open call for contemporary dancers, and I thought you should audition."

"Thanks," Alexandra said, dismayed, "but I can barely walk."

"Look at the clock," Leah said impatiently. "You have half an hour, the pills will have kicked in by then. This business is not for people who make excuses, Alexandra. Besides, I doubt that they will want you to do much, I think it's just for look."

"Okay, okay, okay." Alexandra swallowed two extra-strength Tylenol dry.

"I would've gone for the Aleve myself," Leah said.

"I wouldn't," Alexandra said honestly. "I had some of that stuff when I was in the States during the summer; it really hit me for a loop."

"That's because you are too skinny," Leah complained. She took one hand away from her steering wheel and hit Alexandra's chest.

"Ow," Alexandra complained.

"Women are supposed to have boobs, Alexandra."

"Boobs are gross."

"Have you even had your period yet?"

"Oh my freaking God, Leah! Please don't say period. Like, ever. Ew."

"I'm just asking. Somebody should be. Okay, get out — wait." Leah parked and turned around, beginning to dig through a large pile of dance clothing and costumes in the back seat. "Here. I think these are Anna's. She left them last time she came to take class, so they should fit you." Leah handed Alexandra a pair of black shorts and a sports bra that had been gathered in the middle so that it curved down between the breasts like a normal bra.

"Okay. Thanks."

"No problem. Phone me when you are out, I'll pick you up — you are in no state to walk."

Alexandra gingerly got out of the car. "Or dance. I hope this kicks in soon."

"Here. Take a bottle with you." Leah handed her one of the bottles of Tylenol, and Alexandra began to slowly climb the many steps leading up to Harbour Dance Centre's studios.

As Alexandra walked up she realized that she had forgotten to ask Leah what exactly she was auditioning for. *Oh well. There can't be too many auditions taking place on a Wednesday night at a drop-in dance centre.* She walked up to the desk. "Heeeeey ... I'm here for the audition?"

"Fill this out, hon."

"Thanks." Alexandra took the form with her into the bathroom and got changed, then filled it out. It didn't say much — just that she was auditioning for Trident Dancer. She wondered if she should take her hair down or not. She looked at herself in the mirror. No, better just have it in a ponytail since she didn't know what they would want her to do. She left the change room and went to the studio to wait, starting to stretch. It felt good to be auditioning for something that she didn't feel any pressure about. If there were no expectations, then she didn't have to feel bad if she didn't get it. *Plus*, she thought as she watched the other dancers trickle into the room, *it doesn't look like anyone else is any good.* Her body felt nice, tired but warm and stretched out. If it wasn't for her foot, she'd feel perfect. She stood up and *grand battemented* her foot backwards, high above her head, letting her back sink down in the way that would get her *so* yelled at if she was in ballet class, but was so much fun to do. Down, and up, swinging her leg like the arm on an old grandfather clock.

She sat down, growing bored, and massaged her foot. The people walking in did not look like she had expected. Not like dancers, not like actors. She wasn't quite sure how to classify them in her brain. *A cross between? Actors who could dance? Dancers who could act?* Whoever they were, they were wearing very little clothing. One of them, a pretty blonde who Alexandra thought she might have seen at a jazz class once, was wearing what looked like black underwear and a jean corset. Alexandra was glad that Leah had tossed her some clothing to wear; in her shorts and bra she was almost wearing too much for this audition.

A woman with dyed-blond hair walked in, obviously not auditioning — she was fully clothed and looked to be in her late twenties or early thirties. "Hey girls. Thanks for coming out. If you could all just give me your forms and head shots if you have them?"

Alexandra handed her form to the woman. She didn't have a head shot with her. As she watched the pile stack up, she could see that she was probably the only person without one. *Well, I didn't know I was going to audition today. It's not really that important ... I hope.*

"Okay, just want to give you some background," the woman said, speaking quickly. "So, what is going to happen is you are the spirits of the trident. The hero who steals the trident is not paying attention, and so you come to him and pull his essence out."

Sort of like the willis from Giselle, Alexandra thought to herself. *Taking away his life force.*

"So, we're like, you know, sucking the guy's, like, sex drive out of him?" a brunette in the front asked.

Alexandra's eyebrows flew up higher than Charlie Chaplin's. *What? Where the frick did she get that from?*

"Exactly," the blond woman agreed.

Alexandra's face fell. *What the …?*

"Now, I want you girls to all to learn a small section of the choreography, you can show it to me in groups, and then I want you to all freestyle it across the floor. Any questions? No? Okay, show me what you got."

Alexandra started to learn the choreography, which was a form of burlesque dancing. When it was time to perform it, she went in the group with the blond corset-girl. She knew the choreography, it required no technique at all, but as she was dancing it she realized it was supposed to look completely different from the way she was doing it. She watched the blond girl in the mirror, and as she did, she considered just leaving the room. She was clearly not going to get this. She stayed, because it was an audition, and to leave an audition in the middle would be a bigger breach of protocol than she was capable of. Besides, she was curious. She had almost forgotten about her foot, she realized; the pain-killers must have kicked in, either that or the audition was too entertaining to let her think about it.

Finally it was time to go across the floor, and Alexandra made sure that she was in a different group from the blond girl, so she could watch her. Alexandra started out trying to do the freestyle seriously, but a quarter of the way across the floor embarrassment kicked in and she did a series of extensions instead. If she wasn't going to get the part, at least she could prove to everyone that she was a far better dancer than they were or were ever going to be. *They all look a lot older than me, though.*

"Okay, I think I've got who I want to call back for tomorrow," the woman said, speaking quickly. She called out about ten names, and Alexandra's wasn't one of them. Alexandra wasn't sure how she felt about that. She didn't want it, but she never enjoyed not being picked. It was a very curious sort of mixed feeling: like when that person who always wants to hang out with you — that you don't want to hang out with — stops calling. You still don't want to hang out with them, but you miss being asked. Alexandra walked into the change room and started getting changed. The blond girl was also going to get changed, although she of course had been one of the ten.

"You looked good out there!" she said sweetly.

"Uh, thanks," Alexandra said, not entirely sure what to say since she had clearly *not* been good out there. The obvious thing to do was to compliment the other girl, but she wasn't sure how to do that without being rude. *What am I supposed to say? You'd make a really good stripper?* "I didn't quite realize — like, I felt kind of out of place in there."

"You looked good," the girl said. "Well, like, a little awkward, but your extensions are fricking *amazing!*"

Alexandra laughed, softening up. The easiest way to make friends with Alexandra was to compliment her extensions: she was very proud of them. "Ballet can do that to you."

"Ohhh, ballet girl. That explains it."

"Yeah, at least I didn't come to this audition with a bun in my hair, right?" Alexandra laughed.

The girl looked confused. "Yeah ... that would have been ... bad. I guess I'll see you around."

"For sure. Nice meeting you." Alexandra fled the studio, going down the steps much faster than she had gone up them. She pulled out her cellphone. "Hey, Leah — I'm done."

"I'm outside."

Alexandra pushed open the door and entered the real world, or at least downtown Granville Street in the dark. She walked over to Leah's car and got in.

"How was it? How's your foot?"

"Oh my goddddd, Leah! It was like a fricking stripper audition, I swear! We were supposed to be like these spirit things, but then we were like supposed to suck the —" Alexandra made air quotations with her hands "— *sex drive* out of this dude? Like, seriously, wtf?"

"Well, how did you do?" Leah asked calmly.

"Horribly," Alexandra said gloomily. "Leah, it was the weirdest thing. I have never wanted to be a stripper, but I always thought that, like, you didn't have to be good at it, right? Like, either you were hot, or you weren't. But today there was this girl at the audition, and she was really, really, good. And do you know what? I was actually getting upset because I wouldn't make a good stripper. It was so stupid."

"So you didn't even try," Leah said, sounding a bit annoyed.

"Well, I did *try*," Alexandra said unconvincingly. "Sort of." She bent down and picked up her foot, pulling it up toward her face so that she could look at it. "Agh. It's starting to hurt again."

"You should get your mom to take you to the doctor."

"I will," Alexandra lied.

"*Actually*, Alexandra. And by the way, next time you come to take class, you should bring that new kid at your school."

"Who?"

"Julian."

"I'll see what I can do. Thank you for taking me to the audition and driving me home and stuff, Leah. Sorry I wasn't any good at being a stripper." Alexandra giggled.

"It's fine, Lexi. Turn on the radio?" Adele was on the air with "Set Fire to the Rain," and they both began singing along as Leah drove Alexandra home.

Chapter Ten

Julian Reese
(Dance + School) x No Sleep = Julian wants a day off.
And a cookie :D

"Oh!" A shrill scream disrupted Julian's peaceful rendition of the *develope* exercise they were working on. He looked across the *barre* in the direction of the scream, and dropped his leg. George stopped playing. Everyone stared. Keiko had her hands over her mouth and was staring at the ground. Mao was on the floor. Mrs. Castillo hurried over and rolled her over. "You okay, you okay, you okay?"

"*Hai*," Mao said weakly. "My head ..."

Mrs. Castillo looked over to Keiko. "Go tell Gabriel, bring me some juice, some, chocolate, something." Keiko nodded and ran out of the room.

"What just happened?" Julian asked, leaning across to Jonathon.

"I think she just fainted."

"Oh." Julian stared at Mao as she slowly sat up. Gabriel came hurrying back in, holding a basket of strawberries and some yogurt-covered raisins. "These, these are Mrs. Demidovski's," he said, holding out the bowl to Mao. "Have some. They are very good." He helped her get up and took her out into the hall.

"Okay, everyone, very exciting, I know, but now let's work," Mrs. Castillo said firmly. "George, music, please. We start from beginning again."

During the break, Julian, like almost all of his class, flooded out of the studio and into the waiting room to see if Mao was all right. "Hey, Mao," Julian said, sitting in the seat beside her and tucking his feet up. "You all right?" As she was his homestay sister, he felt as though he had special rights in the area of inquiring after her health. Everyone else was forced to hover curiously around them.

"I'm fine," Mao assured him. "Just forget to eat breakfast, and then — bang!"

"Yeah, we heard," Julian said, giggling despite the seriousness.

"It was funny, wasn't it?" Mao said, smiling.

Gabriel came out of the office and walked toward him. "Mao, can you come here? Mrs. Demidovski wants to talk to you."

"Uh-oh," Tristan said as she left. Everyone else went back into the studio now that the entertainment was gone.

"Why?" Julian asked, frowning. "She looks like she's going to be fine."

"They're probably going to make her go back to Japan."

"Why?" Julian exclaimed.

"Think about it, Jules," Tristan said. "They have to. She fainted because she wasn't eating enough and the academy doesn't want to be accused of ignoring eating disorders. Fainting is pretty obvious."

"But, they won't actually, will they?" Julian asked. "Couldn't they just ask her to eat more?"

Tristan shrugged. "I doubt they will. This is easier. It happened last year, too."

"Somebody fainted?"

"No, it was a bit different." Tristan started to giggle. "It was this girl who was staying with Mr. Yu, actually."

"What happened?"

"Well, I don't know why they made her leave the school. But, anyway, one time me and Kageki were eating this cake we'd bought from Daun's — you know those white cakes that they make, right? With the whipping cream and fruit on top? The ridiculously light and sweet ones?"

"Yeah, they're so gross."

"Kind of, but they look good. Anyway, we were eating it, and then we left, and I set it on top of the garbage can, like, you know, the kind without a lid, so it was pretty full and then there was this cake box just perched on top, right?"

"Okay …?"

"And then Kageki and me went into the studio right next to it, and were like joking around and stuff, but then we decided to go downstairs for some reason so we came out of the studio. And this girl was there, eating the cake out of the garbage, and then she just drops it back in the can, screams, and goes downstairs. Like, seriously. It was the weirdest thing. So gross."

"Wait, what?"

"Exactly! And the thing was she had money. And she never ate her lunch or anything; Leon said that she'd just eat like fifteen oranges every day or something. I remember him going on about it because he said that Mr. Yu had been bugging her about it at dinner, he said that she would turn orange."

"Okay, I don't think that she could turn orange, but that is really weird, and kind of messed up."

"Yeah."

"That doesn't mean that they will make Mao go home. She just fainted."

"In front of everyone. I bet they will."

"That really sucks." They heard the sound of a piano playing in the studio, and quickly ran back in.

Julian got changed quickly after class; he had a huge amount of homework to finish. He was just going up the stairs when Alexandra accosted him. "Hey."

"Hey …?"

"I'm going to go take class at Leah's school tonight. Want to come?"

Julian wavered for approximately three seconds. Homework that would take him all night to finish, or class with Leah? *Definitely class with Leah.* "Just a second, have to go get my shoes and stuff." He ran back down the stairs and opened his locker, digging around in the mess inside for the stuff that he wanted.

Tristan was at his locker getting changed. "What? Julian, did you do this?"

Julian looked over at the dancing stick-figure in a tutu. "Ah, no. Did you just notice that? Andrew Lui did it while he was visiting."

"Oh. That is really random. But cool — Andrew Lui drew on my locker!"

"Hey, I'm finally going to take class with Leah at her studio, want to come? I'm going with Alexandra."

"Uhhhhh … I have so much homework …."

"Me, too, dude. Just come!"

"Okay, *fiiiine.*" Tristan grabbed his shoes and shorts back out of his locker, stuffed them in his bag, and followed Julian out the door.

Justin was waiting in the car. "I thought Mom was picking me up?" Alexandra said, her face falling.

"Nice to see you too, sis," Justin said. "Uh, what's with the entourage?"

"We all wanted to go take Leah's six o'clock class," Tristan answered for her.

"I thought Mom was going to be driving," Alexandra repeated. "Can you drive us?"

Justin groaned. "Alexandra, I have an essay do, a lab to finish, and all my homework problems …"

"We can go another night, that's fine," Tristan said quickly.

"*Please* Justin? It will take you, like, fifteen minutes more," Alexandra said.

"More like half an hour more. Okay. But I'm not picking you up; you'll have to get Mom or Dad to do that."

"Kk." They got in the car, and Justin started to drive toward the east side where Leah's studio was located. He turned the music up loud so that they couldn't talk. They were at the studio in closer to fifteen minutes than thirty, and hopped out fast, Justin unwilling to even park.

"Bye."

"Bye." Justin sped away, and Alexandra shook her head. "He got a ticket last week, he's going to be, like, totally broke if he gets another one. Then how's he going to be able to buy all that rum he drinks?"

"How come you don't look like your brother?" Tristan asked, staring after him.

"Less beer and carbs, more X chromosomes. Also, I have a much better haircut. Come *on,* it's almost six!"

The music was already blaring in the big studio when they stepped in. Tristan peered around the corner. Leah was rehearsing her junior competition company, and they were working on a piece set to a Jessie J song. She saw him and flashed him a thumbs-up. He grinned.

"You taking class, kid?" she yelled across the studio.

"Yes, ma'am!" He left the studio door and ran to catch up with Tristan and Alexandra. They got changed quickly and made their way against the tide of ten- to thirteen-year-olds who were pouring out of the studio. Most of the senior company was already there, stretching on the floor. Leah's students didn't have a special academic program like at the academy, so they all had to take class after school.

Leah motioned Julian over to talk to her. "You finally came," she said.

"Yeah. I said I would!"

"Took you long enough. Now, I wanted to talk to you about something. Alexandra said that you were a choreographer."

"Sort of. Like, I like to choreograph, but I'm not —"

"Don't be stupid. If you choreograph, you are a choreographer. Repeat after me, I. Am. A. Choreographer."

"I am a choreographer."

"Delivery needs work. See that girl over there?" Julian looked in the direction she was pointing, toward a corner full of dancers.

"Uh,there's a lot of girls there."

"That one. The dark-skinned girl with the red shorts and the white knee socks." At that moment the girl looked over at them and smiled. She had the whitest teeth he had ever seen, and he shivered. There was something about the combination of tiredness, fluorescent lighting, and toothpaste-commercial white teeth that freaked the hell out of him.

"Yeah, I see her."

"Listen to me carefully. That girl is really talented. Really. She's older than you, about nineteen now, and she's trying to get a small contemporary company together, doing all the choreography herself."

"Cool."

"She can't do all the choreography because she isn't good enough. Her parents have money and they're willing to fund this. They want their little girl to do what she loves. You understand?"

"Um, not really." Julian stared at her, feeling slightly dizzy, from the lights, the loud music and talking, the bright dance clothing that was completely different from the academy's uniform.

"What I am saying is, go make friends with her. You could really help each other out. Her name is Frida."

"Okay," Julian replied.

Leah stood up and walked to the CD player, and Julian melted back into the crowd of students, all just spread out instead of in the ordered lines that ruled classes at the academy. Leah began the class with a warm-up, which Julian did not need thanks to his already full day of classes before this. It was always a bit painful to stretch again after his body had gotten cold for the day. Leah then led them through a series of fast-paced choreography sequences. Julian kept sneaking glances at Frida, trying to get some clue as to how good she would be at choreography, or at dance in general, but to him, she just looked average. Alexandra was a million times better than her, at everything. She was stronger than Alexandra, at some steps that did not combine flexibility and strength, but that was not very important.

Leah gave them a water break, and Julian sipped slowly, trying not to choke. He found it difficult to drink after he had been dancing; his throat seemed to close up. At the front of the room, Leah looked at him pointedly. Julian gulped. He walked over to the girl, feeling suddenly quite young, and stood beside her, trying to look casual as he considered what he should say. In the end, he didn't have to say anything.

"Hey, I'm Frida," she said, holding out her hand. They awkwardly half-shook, half-clasped hands. "You haven't come to take Leah's class before, have you?"

"No," Julian admitted. "I haven't. I took her class at Harbour, though. And my friends over there have been here a lot." He pointed to Alexandra and Tristan, who were sitting on the floor and kept looking at him.

"Oh … are you from the academy, then?"

"Yes."

"Well, good luck. Nobody here really likes the academy."

"Why?" Julian protested.

Frida shrugged, putting the cap back on her water bottle. "A lot of things … an inferiority complex, the fact that we think everyone at the academy is stuck on themselves and anorexic, the fact that Leah always gives lectures on how the academy can make you hate dancing, kill the joy of it for you."

"That's not true," Julian said, quick to leap to the defence of his school.

Frida shrugged. "I've never been there, so …"

Julian decided to be blunt. It seemed the easiest, and he was tired. "Leah told me to talk to you. She was telling me about how you wanted to start your own contemporary company."

Frida's face lit up, and she showed her dimples along with more perfectly white teeth. Julian wondered if her parents were both dentists. "I know who you are now! You're that boy from the Island. Leah was telling me about you, because I've been trying to figure out who I want on board with me, in this company, I mean, of course, and it's all sort of been turning into a nightmare."

"Well, of course," Julian said, laughing. "It's the arts. Anything in the arts that's worth doing is going to be a nightmare. If it's smooth, you know you're not making art."

Frida stared at him. "How old are you? I'm sorry, I don't know your name."

"Julian Reese. I'm sixteen."

"Frida Levesque. I'm nineteen. You seem very mature for your age."

"That's because I'm tired. It makes me calm and I start to act normal. You just don't want to meet me when I'm awake."

"Oh. I see."

Leah clapped her hands. "Hey! Everyone. Teatime's over. We're going to do improv tonight, okay? Get into pairs." Julian looked over at Alexandra and Tristan, but they were already standing next to each other.

"Want to go with me?" Frida asked, smiling. She was the sort of person that nobody ever said no to, and although that kind of confidence was annoying on most people, it suited her.

"Sure," Julian agreed, relieved that he didn't have to search around for a partner. Leah turned on the music, a sort of folk-instrumental sound, and they began. Leah's philosophy toward improv was to keep in contact, and that is what Julian and Frida did, starting with hands and moving onward. *From the outside*, Julian couldn't help thinking, *this would look incredibly awkward.* But, it just wasn't. It was normal. It fit Julian's theory that the human body was whatever you wanted it to be. It was like how the naked body could be pornographic, art, or just another nude person at Wreck Beach. The same body could mean a completely different thing in each context. So, they danced. Frida was different to dance with than Alexandra had been during Leah's class in Spring Break. Where Alexandra would just move away to do something by herself if she didn't like where Julian was taking their movement, Frida would force him to go in the direction she wanted. She was just stronger. The power balance was different. It took Julian a bit to get used to, but after about a minute he had adjusted, and their movements became very in tune.

The last notes of the song died away, and Leah clapped her hands. "Good, everyone. Julian, Frida, very *simpatico*, nice work."

After they had finished, Julian got changed next to Tristan, but Tristan was oddly quiet. They went out into the hall to find Alexandra.

"Hey." Frida was sitting on the bench in the hall. "Trade numbers? I'll let you know if anything goes down, you can decide then if you want to be involved."

Alexandra and Tristan stood behind him as he traded numbers with her, and Julian was awkwardly conscious of them watching. "I'll add you on Facebook, too," Frida said, smiling at him. "I really hope I can get you involved on something soon — it's just, first we need the something that you could be involved on."

"Yeah." Julian laughed. "Okay. Nice meeting you. Bye."

The three of them walked out, Tristan and Alexandra walking very tightly on either side of him. Tight as in Julian had difficulty walking without stepping on their toes. "What was that?" Alexandra asked at the same time that Tristan said, "I've never seen you try and act professional before."

Julian shrugged, embarrassed. "Did I really look like I was trying to act professional?" he asked Tristan.

"It wasn't *that* bad," Tristan relented. "It's just because we know you that we noticed."

"Oh. Good," Julian said, relieved. They started walking to the bus loop. Leah's studio was in the middle of low-income suburban nothingness, and there was shop after empty shop along the street, the kind that sells windows, or carpet-cleaning services. At the end of the street there was an empty bus loop and a McDonald's.

"What's the story, then?" Alexandra demanded impatiently, looping her arm in his. Tristan did the same on the other side. Julian decided his friends were strange.

"Leah told me that Frida was trying to start up a small contemporary company," Julian said uncomfortably, highly aware that Leah had told him, who she barely knew, and not Alexandra and Tristan. "I think it was because you told her that I liked choreographing, Alexandra."

Alexandra frowned. "*Frida* is starting a contemporary company? But she isn't any good. Well, she's okay, but not brilliant."

Julian yawned. "I don't know, dude."

They sat at the bus bench and Alexandra phoned her parents, trying to get them to pick up and give her a ride home. "Ugh!" she said after finally getting through to them. "They want me to bus back to downtown; they said they would pick me up there."

"Uh —" Tristan said pointedly.

Alexandra sighed. "Yes, you may sleep over Tristan.

But you're not borrowing a shirt. You got tomato soup all over that white one of mine last time."

"Yay. There are, like, no buses near my home," Tristan explained to Julian. Julian nodded; it was getting close to ten o'clock and it was probably going to take him close to an hour to get home since all the buses that he needed to take stopped running frequently at this time of night.

They got on the almost-empty bus. The bus driver made them all show their student ID to prove that they qualified for their bus passes, looking suspicious. *Geez*, Julian thought impatiently, *does he really have nothing better to do?* If he were a bus driver, he would never check that sort of stuff. It was the kind of thing that could be left for the transit police to do. The bus went on its way, stopping to let only a few people get on or off each stop, and Julian fell half-asleep, leaning his head on Alexandra's shoulder as Tristan did the same to him.

By the time Julian got home, the clock on the kitchen microwave said it was eleven. Which meant it was probably about ten minutes past eleven, or maybe a quarter to. Julian grabbed his dinner out of the fridge and took it to his room to eat. He could see all of the homework he had to do, spread out all over the room, but he was too tired to even pick it up and sort it out, let alone actually do it. Instead, he picked up Theresa's biography and continued reading it. He was almost at the chapter that talked about Isaac, but he was trying to force himself to read it in order. He ate his green vegetables and ham and mashed potatoes slowly, as he read about the first time Theresa guested in Belgium.

Chapter Eleven

Kaitlyn Wardle
Watching The Big Bang Theory with my mom — so cool :p

Kaitlyn spun around in front of the mirror, trying to see her butt. It had to look smaller; she had lost five pounds. *Okay, I just can't see it*, she decided.

"Kaitlyn, come on!" Jeff yelled from downstairs. "You are going to be late for school."

"Coming …" Kaitlyn picked up her backpack and ran downstairs, joining her father in his car.

"How's school?" Jeff asked. He had a set of questions that he asked while he drove her to school, and asking about school was one of them. Along with, "How is your peer group rating?" a question he found hilarious because it was taken from an old *Peanuts* cartoon, and "How is dance?"

"School's good."

"Really? Have you had that course-planning session with your counsellor yet?"

"Not yet, Dad. I know what I'm going to put down, though."

"Have you thought about what you are going to take in grade eleven and twelve yet?"

"Not really."

"Do you have any idea what you would like to take in university if you go?"

"Nope."

"You could always go to university to take dance, I suppose," Jeff said, thinking.

"Dad, that's totally stupid. You aren't going to be dancing for a good ballet company if you are going to university for dance. If I ever went to university, it would definitely be for something academic."

"Okay. That makes sense."

"It's a while before I have to think about this, anyway."

"It's coming faster than you think, Kaitlyn. But okay. Have a good day." She climbed out of his car and began walking up to the doors of McKinley Secondary. She was tired of thinking about her future. Discussions on the topic both scared and bored her. She pushed open the doors and walked toward a round table that had been taken over by a group of Super Achievers students.

"Hey guys."

They ignored Kaitlyn, the decibel level of their conversation too high to even hear her. She sat down next to Cromwell Gilly. McKinley let him put on a fashion show each spring, a half-hour show where students wearing his work paraded down a long runway he created down the steps inside the school.

"Sweetie, just wait till you see her dress. Bright yellow to bring out her hair, bits of blue — sweetheart, there's even a *train*." He was talking to Sasha, a rhythmic gymnast, about Taylor's dress. *Of course he's getting Taylor to model for him*, Kaitlyn thought, jealous, but agreeing with his choice. If she was a designer she would want Taylor to model her stuff, too.

Keiko came up to them, looking perfect as always. Kaitlyn wasn't sure how she always managed to look so calm and ordered. Her clothes always matched, she did her makeup perfectly, and she apparently had gotten up early enough this morning to bring a thermos of tea. "Keiko! Sweetheart, you're still going to be in my show? Right? Right?"

"Of course," Keiko said, smiling. "Be calm, Cromwell Gilly, I said I will do."

"Okay, you are going to just die so dead when you see what I made for you. I have been working my fingers to the bone for it. At first, I was like, I can't make you a kimono-themed dress. That's racist. And then I was like, why is that racist? It's fricking brilliant! You are going to love it."

"Okay."

Julian collapsed at the bench beside them, buried his head in his arms, and promptly had to lift his head again so that he could yawn.

"Good morning, *sunshine!* What have you been up to, sweetheart?"

"Dancing. Reading," Julian mumbled from the depths of his elbow.

"Want to be a part of high fashion?"

"If I have to. Do I get to do my own makeup?" Julian suddenly sat up, an expression of unholy glee on his face. "I'll do it if I can put on my makeup."

"No. I don't trust you."

"Fine. Cromwell Gilly, do you know what would make your show even better?"

"Two of me?"

"No. One of you is enough. Imagine if instead of having your iPod playlist on while they're coming down the runway, you played the drums."

"Absolutely not. I'll be way too busy."

"Fine, fine … I still think it might be cool, though. And like, you could have everyone dance once they reached the bottom? It would be so sweet."

"Jules. Look at me, sweetheart. Do I look like I want to put on musicals? No."

"Oh! I didn't even think of that. Of course you should have one of the opera singers join in too. They could be singing like … like … 'Lucy in the Sky with Diamonds.' Your dresses always remind me of that song. Are you okay, Cromwell Gilly?"

Cromwell Gilly gulped. "Jules, somewhere in that ocean of idiocy is a genius trying not to drown. That is the name of my show. It's perfect."

"What?"

"*Lucy in the Sky with Diamonds*. That's the theme of this show. It's so perfect!"

"Glad I could help." Julian put his head back down and promptly fell asleep.

Kaitlyn was up and out of her seat the second the bell rang. She had thought that Taylor was annoying in class with her incessant talking, fidgeting, and texting, but the alternative was apparently absolute boredom. She had no one to talk with in class now, and nothing to do but doodle, which — because she was painfully bad at drawing — was extremely unsatisfactory. She hurried out into the hall, doing up her jacket, and was accosted by Jessica and Jonathon. "Hey, hey, stop, kid," Jonathon said. "I heard that Mr. Angelo was handing out the yearbooks early to Super Achievers students. Come on, let's go get ours."

"Okay," Kaitlyn said. They ran up the next flight of stairs to where the English classrooms were and down the hall to Mr. Angelo's classroom.

Somebody was already there, talking to Mr. Angelo. They stopped outside, realizing that it was Alexandra. He was talking quietly and they couldn't hear what he was saying. "Let's just go in," Kaitlyn said impatiently. "Come on, we're going to miss the bus." Kaitlyn walked into the classroom and Jessica and Jonathon followed her. "Oh." *Crap.* Alexandra was holding a pile of journals and her yearbook, and she looked like she had been crying.

"Be with you in minute, guys," Mr. Angelo said quickly. "So, Alexandra, you can handle this for me? It's a bit out of the proper procedure — if there is a procedure for this sort of thing — but I think it would be better coming from you."

Alexandra nodded.

"Okay then. I should probably put them in a sealed envelope —" Mr. Angelo dug around on his messy desk and found a large brown envelope. He put one of the journals that Alexandra was holding inside, carefully licked it and closed it. On the outside he wrote FOR MRS. CASTILLO in Sharpie, and then marked the date. He paused and looked at Alexandra. "Do you think I should also put my phone number? In case she wants to ask me something?"

"Yes," Alexandra said decisively.

"All right. Thank you for handling this for me, Lexi. And if you ever change your mind about helping out with the newsletter, or just want to contribute to a small section of it, let me know."

"Okay. Thanks, Mr. Angelo."

"Now, you guys, here for yearbooks, am I right? All of you are in Super Achievers, no fakers? Last year I got in trouble with Mr. Murray because I let some regular students get theirs early, and that apparently led to anarchy." Mr. Angelo chuckled at his own wit and gave Kaitlyn, Jessica, and Jonathon their yearbooks.

They took them quickly and ran for the bus; just as they ran up to the stop, the bus pulled out. "Really? Really?" Jonathon complained. "He totally saw us. That bus driver hates us."

"Jonathon, the bus driver does not hate you," Jessica sighed.

"What was that about?" Kaitlyn asked Alexandra quietly as Jessica and Jonathon continued to argue.

Alexandra shook her head. "Mr. Angelo wanted to talk to me about writing an article that focuses on things that the Super Achievers students were doing. I haven't decided yet if I have time to do it, though."

"What about the envelope?"

"You know those journals that they make us keep at the beginning of class?"

"Yes …?" Kaitlyn said, not sure where Alexandra was going with this.

"Well, I'd forgotten to pick up my journals from grade ten, so I went by to pick them up."

"What? They were still there? Alexandra, that's, like, a year."

"Yeah, he has a whole filing cabinet of old journals that people had left. Like, really old ones. And he found mine, and then he found one left by Mrs. Castillo's daughter."

"Mrs. Castillo had a daughter?" Kaitlyn exclaimed. She had never thought of Mrs. Castillo having a daughter. She didn't seem like the sort of person who would have children. "I didn't even know she was married."

"What do you think the *Mrs.* is for?" Alexandra said sarcastically.

"Oh. Yeah, I guess that makes sense. But where is her husband, then?"

"Still in Cuba, I think. Mrs. Castillo came over here with her daughter when the Demidovskis gave her a job, and her husband couldn't come. I'm not sure why."

"So … where is her daughter?"

"Um … she was in a car accident in England, several years ago. She died."

Kaitlyn stared at her, realizing now why that journal was such a big deal. "Oh, geez."

"Exactly." The next bus pulled up to the bus stop, and they got on.

"Sign my yearbook?" Jessica asked Alexandra.

"Later," Alexandra snapped. "We can all sign at the academy." Kaitlyn stared out the window. She couldn't picture having Mrs. Castillo as a mother.

The academy was suffering the effects of a full year with not enough sun, and when the sun finally came out, it highlighted all of the dirt and grime coating the building, inside and out.

"Seriously, has anyone found out if they have a janitor yet?" Kaitlyn complained.

"Just clean it yourself if it bothers you so much," Jonathon said, irritated.

Taylor came up to Kaitlyn, a huge smile on her face. "Sign mine?"

"Wait, how did you get a yearbook? You don't even go to McKinley anymore."

"Yeah, but I paid my school fees. I got Angela to bring mine for me."

"Okay …" Kaitlyn sat down on the floor and traded yearbooks with Taylor.

Taylor handed her a sparkly green gel pen to write her message. "I'm getting everyone to write in a different colour," she explained.

"Um, okay …"

"What colour do you want me to write for yours?"

"Um, up to you."

"I'm going to do it in this pink one then. I call one of the blank pages in the back."

"Okay." Kaitlyn started to write. *Hey, Tay, it's been great dancing with you this year! HAGS, love you. Kaitlyn.* She looked up; Taylor was still writing. And writing. And writing. "Hey, when do you think you will be finished, Taylor? I want to get other people to sign, too, before class starts."

"'I'll be done soon," Taylor said absently. "I'm trying to describe our year so that you can remember it. How do you spell 'oranges'?"

"*O-R-A-N-G-E-S*, I think. Okay, you can keep my book for a bit, I'm going to go get changed."

"Okay." Kaitlyn left Taylor and went downstairs. There was a commotion in the girl's change room, and she began to walk faster, not wanting to miss whatever was happening.

There was a circle around Mao, who was sitting on the bench, crying. "What's wrong?" Kaitlyn asked.

"She has to go home," Keiko said sadly. "And she doesn't want to. She doesn't want to work in Japanese ballet company, she wants to work in Canadian ballet company, and if she leaves, where will she go?"

"Oh." Kaitlyn stood there awkwardly. She wasn't close to Mao. "Aren't they at least going to let her finish up the year?"

"Yes, but she can't come back in September."

"Mao, I'm sorry. Maybe you can still get a job in Canada."

Mao shook her head, tears rolling down her face. "Not easy," she said. Kaitlyn got changed quickly and headed upstairs, wanting to get away from the awkwardness.

Upstairs, Aiko had dropped by and was being hugged to death in the hallway by everyone along with Leon. Mr. Yu was going to give her a ride to the airport later, she was telling Alexandra. Kaitlyn was surprised to see that Alexandra looked extremely choked up about Aiko leaving.

"I remember when you first came to Canada," Dimitri said, sprawled out on one of the chairs, laughing at the fuss. "You were so cute, but you got lost all the time!"

"Oh … I forget that," Aiko laughed. "Yes, I always used to get lost, 'where is bathroom?' 'where is bus stop?', 'help, how I get home?'"

Dimitri laughed. "Yup. That's how I'm going to remember you."

"Please, no," Aiko said firmly. "Now I don't get lost … so much. Now I can read English!"

Kaitlyn giggled. "When did you come here, Aiko?" she asked, curious.

"When I was thirteen," Aiko said, smiling. "Now I am eighteen — I am old."

"You came here when you were thirteen? Wow, I didn't know that." Kaitlyn thought about that. She couldn't picture going to Japan by herself when she was thirteen and not being able to read the signs or understand the other students. She also couldn't picture her mother ever letting her try.

"Good luck," Tristan said, hugging her and Leon.

"Time to go, time to go," Mr. Yu said impatiently, walking over. "You want to miss plane?" He looked at Tristan and winked. "When you get job, uh? Soon? You getting old …"

"Er … working on it," Tristan said uncomfortably. Aiko and Leon disappeared out the door.

But Aiko suddenly ran back. She handed Alexandra a hair pin shaped like a flower. "Here, a present," she said, smiling. "You are the best at the academy now. *Ganbate!*"

"*Ganbate*," Alexandra said, in shock, as Aiko ran out. She looked down at the pin in her hand, and Kaitlyn gulped. She would have given a whole lot to have been the one that Aiko said that to. *What about Grace …?* Kaitlyn looked across the room; Grace's expression as she stared at Alexandra looked as upset as Kaitlyn felt.

"Everyone, are you coming to class today? Or is this a Canadian holiday somebody forgot to tell me about?" Mr. Moretti said impatiently, standing in the doorway. They all quickly went into the studio.

"I know everyone is very excited for summer," Mr. Moretti said, cracking his back against the *barres*. "But this is not summer yet. You will have to put up with me for a few more weeks yet, babies. Come on, to work."

Kaitlyn sighed and began to work. The summer sun was just teasing them, shining through the windows and illuminating the dust in the air. Mr. Yu came inside the studio, dragging a piece of the prop house. He walked back outside the door and came back with a large bucket of paint. He loudly dragged the house over to the wall so that it was propped up, and began to paint, whistling noiselessly.

"Do you really have to always do this here?" Mr. Moretti said, annoyed. "Always? Really, it is enough!"

"This is the biggest studio," Mr. Yu explained.

"I don't see your point. You fail to make sense, my little man." Kaitlyn was a little confused by this comment, because it was so blatantly untrue. Mr. Yu was very tall.

They were working on an *adagio* exercise, when Kaitlyn felt a sharp jab in her back. "Ow! What …?"

It was Taylor. "Look," she said, pointing toward the corner of the group that was currently dancing.

In the left corner, in the front, Angela was crying as she danced. As in, red face, tears streaming down face, snot, the entire Broadway production. "Oh dear," Kaitlyn said, dismayed. There wasn't really anything much else to say. Angela kept dancing. Kaitlyn looked over at Mr. Moretti; she distinctly saw him notice (he could hardly miss it) and look away. *I don't blame him; I think I'd do the same. Wtf?!* Angela finished the exercise and stood in the corner, continuing to cry. A couple of the dancers looked over and then quickly looked away; but nobody was friends with Angela, not particularly, and she was not in a very attractive state.

"Why doesn't she just go downstairs to the bathroom if she wants to cry?" Kaitlyn whispered to Taylor. "Like any normal person?"

Taylor shrugged. "I don't know. Come on; let's go ask her what's wrong." Kaitlyn followed Taylor over to Angela. "Angela, let's go outside," Taylor said bossily, taking her by the arm. She led her out into the hall, Mr. Moretti making no comment on them leaving. *He's probably just glad that we are taking care of it*, Kaitlyn thought.

"Here," Kaitlyn said, handing Angela a Kleenex. Angela took it and blew her nose, loudly. Kaitlyn couldn't help looking revolted. Angela did not have one of those rare faces that looked charming when crying; she had the kind that turned red and swollen, plus her mascara had started to run.

"What's wrong?" Taylor asked gently. Taylor liked it

when someone else was having a breakdown; it gave her a rare chance to look confident and give advice.

"It's just … everything!" Angela wailed.

"Well, what is 'everything'?" Kaitlyn asked impatiently.

"Um, well, my parents are coming to see *Coppelia*, and they've invited all their friends, and I don't even know if I am actually going to be in the show."

"What do you mean?" Taylor asked, frowning. "Everyone's in the show."

"I'm just understudying. Understudying one cast." Angela started to cry again, and Kaitlyn passed her another Kleenex. She was starting to get the hang of her new role of Kleenex dispenser. She felt like one of those old nobles during King Louis XIV's reign that Alexandra had been babbling about on the bus, the ones that had jobs like holding the king's wig in the morning. Alexandra had liked him because she said that he was into ballet, and that his most famous mistress, Madame Pompadour, was very, very pretty.

"Oh. Well, I am sure that you will be in it," Taylor reassured her, basing this comment on absolutely nothing. "What else is wrong?"

"I came here to get better at ballet," Angela said through her tears, "but I haven't gotten one single correction since before Christmas."

Taylor and Kaitlyn looked at each other. "That can't possibly be true," Kaitlyn said quickly. "They must've corrected you."

"No," Angela wailed. "Not. One. Single. Correction. How am I supposed to get better that way?"

Taylor and Kaitlyn both sat down on the floor in front of Angela, trying to think of when was the last time that they had heard or seen Angela receive a correction. After a few seconds of thinking, Kaitlyn was forced to concede that what Angela had said might be true. "Oh, wow."

"Exactly," Angela said, wiping her eyes and spreading the mascara a little farther down her face.

"Wow," Kaitlyn repeated. She didn't really know what to say about that. Other than the fact that all the students at the academy had sort of thought that Angela would have quit by now.

"I'm really considering quitting dance," Angela said, breaking down again.

Good idea. You really suck. "Well, have you tried talking to the teachers?"

Angela shrugged. "I've tried," she said. "But I don't know how to. I ask them to correct me, they just say 'must improve,' but they don't say what to improve."

Everything.

Angela stood up. "I think I'm going to go home now. Thanks for making me feel better."

"No problem," Taylor and Kaitlyn said at the same time.

"Get better," Taylor told her, hopping up and giving her a hug. "Eat chocolate. Drink tea."

Angela laughed wetly. "I don't think chocolate is going to help, I'll just feel worse because then I'll be fatter, too. Okay, see you guys tomorrow." She walked off, heading downstairs to get changed.

"Awkward much?" Kaitlyn said.

"Poor Angela," Taylor agreed. They went back to class.

Chapter Twelve

Taylor Audley
Coppelia!!!! So excited!!!! And my dad's coming to watch ...

Taylor was putting on her blush when she heard the shouting. She turned and looked toward the source of the noise in the hall.

"What's that?" Alexandra asked from across the room. They both ran to the door to check. The sight that greeted them was sufficiently odd to reward their effort. Mr. Demidovski and Mr. Moretti were having an argument in the hallway, and they were too absorbed in their fight to notice who was watching them.

"You can't use Jonathon! He can't dance. I have put too much effort into this *bloody* show to see it ruined by that rural idiot!"

"You *can't* use Julie. He has not been rehearsed. He has not had the practice. He is too young."

"Well, that's not my fault, is it? I told you that casting Dimitri was a risk. I told you that Jonathon could not do it. Even Theresa agrees with me, and God knows I hate to agree with that vile woman on anything."

"Julian cannot do!"

"He has to!"

"I will not have it! I am the director! I pay you!"

"You …you *perfetto imbecille!*" Mr. Moretti reached out and pushed Mr. Demidovski to the stage wall. Taylor screamed. Now, pushing someone against the wall in a fit of anger is, while ill-advised, not generally considered that big a deal. But the circumstances take on a more serious tone when the pusher is in their thirties and the pushed is in their seventies. Mr. Moretti looked up at Taylor's scream, and suddenly appeared to realize the inappropriateness of his behaviour. Mr. Demidovski seemed to be in shock, leaning against the wall.

"All right," Mr. Moretti said suddenly. "You can have Jonathon dance the part. I don't care. But I am leaving. I have had enough of this bloody school, this bloody city with its rain, its idiocies, its hockey. I quit." He strode down the hall, walking past Taylor and Alexandra without acknowledging them, although they were staring at him.

"Get me Mr. Yu," Mr. Demidovski said, in a quiet, serious voice that Taylor had never heard before. "And Julian. And Mrs. Demidovski." Taylor and Alexandra nodded and hurried off to do as he asked.

Julian was in the alleyway, texting Frida.

> Yeah, we have our show today, so I can't … but I def can meet up w u on the weekend before I go to the Island :D

He looked up; someone was coming down the alleyway.

"Hey," the person called out.

"Hey," Julian answered neutrally. He opened the door in order to disappear inside the theatre. Only a drunk person would try to make friends with a stranger in an alleyway. *Or ...* Julian took a second look.

"It's me. You forget fast, child." Nat walked up to the door, his hat perched at a rakish angle on his head, complementing his cheery face. "What up, young grass-hopper?" Despite the fact that he was sixteen and a product of the twenty-first century, Nat sometimes liked to mimic the affectations of an upper-class gentleman from the Victorian era.

Julian stared at him blankly, at a loss for words. "I thought you were in Hawaii right now," he said. "You said in Seattle that you were going back there."

Nat shrugged. "Things change. Planes were meant to be flown. Or 'flied'? Or ... you know what, never mind. I'm here, it's a miracle. Let me pass."

Julian stepped back, confused. "*Why* are you here?"

"Never you mind." Nat looked at his cellphone, in the manner of a person who has expected something to happen, and when said something has not happened, searches for answers on their phone.

It was unnecessary, however; Tristan came hurrying up, beaming. "Hey," he said shyly.

Julian stared at them, completely lost.

Tristan looked at him.

"Oh!" The world clicked into place with a bang. *Nat*

and Tristan totally like each other! Julian felt ridiculously pleased with himself for figuring this out. *This is why Nat showed up at the audition for ABT!* He looked at Tristan, who was looking at him like he could make him disappear if he only stared hard enough. "Well, that's great!" Julian suddenly remembered that he had other places to be. "Cool! Like … *really* cool. Sweet. Okay. Bye." He left down the hall, grinning to himself, a boy on a mission: to find Alexandra and give her first dibs on gossip that he really hoped that she didn't already know. He met Alexandra halfway down the hall. "Lexi! Guess what? Nat is here and —"

Alexandra was not listening. "Dimitri isn't dancing. Mr. Moretti doesn't want Jonathon to do it, he wants you to."

Julian's face went white. "What?"

"Yeah. Mr. Demidovski wants to see you."

"What happened to Dimitri?"

"I don't know. Mr. Demidovski and Mr. Moretti were having a big fight, because Mr. Demidovski was saying that you weren't rehearsed, and Mr. Moretti was saying that you needed to be the one because he did not want Jonathon to do it."

"Mr. Demidovski is right. I'm not rehearsed."

"Um, you sort of are," Taylor pointed out. "You've been rehearsing with me."

"Yeah, but that's with you," Julian pointed out. "I've never done it with Alexandra or Grace, and they are the ones dancing."

"Well, nobody said you were dancing yet," Alexandra pointed out "Come *on*, Mr. Demidovski wants you!"

The three of them ran down the long hall to find Mr. Demidovski. Mrs. Demidovski and Mr. Yu were already there, and Mr. Yu looked upset. "Cannot do," he was saying. "No rehearsal, no dress rehearsal, no practice with Lexi or Grace."

"Yes," Mrs. Demidovski agreed. "Must be Jonathon."

Julian stood there, waiting for them to notice that he was there. He did not know which way that he wished they'd decide; it would be incredible to play the part of Frantz, but not like this, not without rehearsal.

"Julian." Tristan's voice echoed from down the hall. "Dude, someone's here to see you." Everyone looked up, confused.

Julian walked down the hall to see who it was. "Hey, I thought I'd drop by to see you," Theresa said, smiling at him. "Are you all right? You look a little unwell."

"Hello, Theresa," Mr. Yu said, nodding formally at her.

Theresa looked around, confused. "Am I interrupting something again?"

Mr. Demidovski raised one dramatic finger. "Theresa," he said slowly. "Do you think Julian could dance the part of Frantz? Or must it be Jonathon?"

Theresa looked absolutely horrified. "Have Jonathon dance the part? He can't! His face, it's so ugly! It is practically in *The Phantom of the Opera* territory." She looked at Julian. "Of course you can do it, can't you, Julian?"

Julian nodded, with a pause between Theresa's words and his nod that drastically undercut the believability of the gesture.

"There, you see? Of course it must be Jonathon."

Mr. Yu frowned. "He has never rehearsed with Lexi, or Grace …"

"Julian, you do," Mr. Demidovski said, fast like someone ripping off a Band-Aid. "Everyone, go get ready for dress rehearsal."

Kaitlyn was getting dressed in the *corps* change room when she heard someone crying in the bathroom. She knocked on the door. "Is everything okay?"

"Yeah." Grace opened the door. "It's just … my parents aren't getting divorced anymore."

Kaitlyn frowned, sure that she must be missing something. "What? Isn't that a good thing?"

"Well, yeah, I guess, but my dad was totally going to move to Sydney, and then I would have gotten to visit Sydney a lot, or, like, move there! They have dance schools there."

"Um …"

"Like, I know that sounds really bad, but that's why I'm upset."

"Okay … how long have they been back together now?"

Grace looked at her cellphone. "Well, they weren't together when I was eating breakfast, because they were fighting then, and I saw them kissing about ten minutes ago, so I guess sometime between then?"

"Well, they might break up again then."

"I hope so! They said that it was me dancing that reminded them how much they loved each other. And then my mom started going on about how when they knew they were having a little girl they were both like 'she's going to be a ballerina!' because like my mom used to dance, and my dad's mom used to dance. And then my dad started talking about destiny."

"That sounds horrible." *I'm glad my parents aren't fricking crazy.*

"Kaitlyn!"

Kaitlyn turned around to see Cecelia standing in front of her. "Yeah, Mom?"

"I brought you your lunch. Why isn't your hair done yet? And did you put your *pointe* shoes in a safe place?"

"Yes."

"So, what I told your Auntie Lynn and Grandma is that you decided you wanted to be in the *corps* because your foot was really bad, okay?"

"Mom!" Kaitlyn said pointedly, gesturing with her head toward the bathroom stall. The bathroom door closed slowly, a hand reaching from the inside to pull it shut.

"Oh. Sorry," Cecelia said in a loud whisper. "Here you are. Do you want me to do your eyeliner for you?"

"Mom! No, I'm good. Thanks." Cecelia continued to hover. "Mom … you are making me kind of nervous. Could you please go and wait in the audience?"

Cecelia looked at her, hurt. "What? You're only dancing in the *corps*, anyway, Kaitlyn!"

"Yeah, it's worse! Mom, I've never danced in the *corps* before. You have to match the timing of all the other dancers, and keep in line, and all the steps are small and stupid."

"Okay. Fine. I'm going to go get a coffee then, you get ready. Have a good rehearsal."

"Bye." Kaitlyn let her breath out as her mother finally left.

The bathroom stall slowly opened again. "Hey," Grace said. "Want me to do your eyeliner?"

"Yes, please!" Kaitlyn said eagerly. "I really suck at it."

Grace perched on the makeup counter and took out Kaitlyn's eyeliner pencil and her liquid eyeliner bottle. She carefully began to draw a smooth line on Kaitlyn's eyelid with the pencil. "By the way, I know who drenched your *pointe* shoes in water during *Nutcracker*."

"Who?" Kaitlyn exclaimed. She managed to not open her eyelids despite her surprise.

"Jessica."

"But why?"

Grace shrugged. "She's a freak. Like, we're friends, I love her, but she's a total freak. And she really hated you."

"I didn't even talk to her."

"I think that's sort of the point? She thought you were super stuck-up. And she was jealous because you got cast so well right away. Now she's okay with you though, obviously."

Kaitlyn gulped. If failing was what it took for Jessica to not hate her she'd rather that Jessica hated her.

Grace finished with the liquid eyeliner. "There. Perfect."

Kaitlyn peered in the mirror. "That's perfect! Thanks. How do you know how to do it so well?"

Grace shrugged. "I started doing my stage makeup for myself when I was nine," she explained. "And I think

I started practising when I was six. So, I've had a lot of experience. We should probably get to the stage, they are probably going to start run-through soon."

Taylor was sitting in the audience watching while Alexandra and Julian kept going through the *pas de deux*. Julian was having trouble, because Alexandra took a little longer on every step than Taylor did.

Tristan suddenly popped into the seat beside Taylor. "Hey."

"Hey to you!" Taylor laughed. "So … Julian told me you and Nat, hey? How'd you manage to keep that a secret?"

"I guess I just forgot to tell you guys."

"So, where is he now?"

"Gone to get some food, he's coming back to watch the matinee."

"Oh. Are you still doing the matinee? I thought they would switch the casts, have Jules do the matinee, you do the evening show."

"They can't. I'm doing the flower *pas de deux* in the evening show, and to switch that all around would be too much. This way it's only Julian and Alexandra who are affected." They both turned to watch Julian and Alexandra rehearse. "He might do okay," Tristan said, surprised. "I didn't think he actually knew it."

"He didn't," Taylor said, frowning. "He's a fast learner when he wants to be."

"Did you manage to find out what happened to Dimitri yet?"

Taylor started to giggle, and could not stop. "Yes."

"What happened?"

"He completely forgot to deal with his immigration stuff. Apparently they had been sending him letters for months, and he had just been ignoring them. He had to get his visa renewed or something. Mr. Yu made Cromwell Gilly drive him somewhere to deal with it this morning, because they had started to call Mr. Yu since Dimitri used to homestay with him."

"Oh geez. Mr. Demidovski is going to kill him when he comes back."

"Yeah."

"Is it just me, or is Alexandra dancing a little off?"

Taylor watched for a few seconds, frowning. "You're right. She is."

Tristan swore. "I bet it's her foot again."

"I think she's okay — look, she did that *arabesque* normally."

Alexandra felt like crying. Not only was she not used to dancing with Julian, but her foot was killing her. Every time she stepped up on *pointe,* she was not sure if it would support her. She was sure that she could do it, if only they stopped rehearsing until the show. "One more time," Mr. Demidovski called out.

Mr. Yu held up his hand, walking over to her. "Okay?" he asked tersely. "Foot okay?"

Alexandra shook her head, swallowing back tears. "No."

"Okay for show?"

"Yes. I just need to go ice it, take some Tylenol."

"Okay." Mr. Yu walked back to Mr. Demidovski and they conferred for a moment. "Okay. Finish," Mr. Yu said, waving. "*Corps* come, run through now." Alexandra and Julian walked off stage, and Alexandra sat down on one of the audience seats, rubbing her foot angrily as if she could bully it into not hurting.

"I'll go get you some ice," Julian said, watching her nervously.

Taylor was dancing the Villagers' waltz when she felt a firm hand push her out of the dance. In the large *corps*, Mr. Yu, of course, did not notice what happened; instead, he just saw Taylor falling out of formation. "Taylor! No mistake!"

Taylor burned with the indignity of it all. She had not made a mistake; stupid Jessica had pushed her. She waited for a second and then rejoined the dance. All went well for a few moments, and then it happened again. "

"Taylor! One more time, I kick you outta the dance." They finished the dance and ran offstage.

Taylor stepped in front of Jessica, brave for once. "You pushed me," she said loudly. Around them, people stopped to watch.

"What are you talking about?" Jessica brushed her off, starting to walk away.

"You pushed me!" Taylor said, getting angry. "In the middle of the dance! And then *I* got in trouble for it."

"You're crazy," Jessica said flatly. She walked back-stage, and Taylor was left with two options: to follow her, and actually look crazy; or to drop it. Taylor dropped it, but it burned.

The matinee had started, and Kaitlyn was sitting backstage watching Grace dance Swanhilda, when she realized something that she maybe should have fully realized sooner. She had never been part of a *corps* before. She had never had to work on a team or take more than a superficial interest in what the other dancers around her were doing. She had never even worn a costume as ill-fitting as the one she currently had on and have it genuinely not matter because the audience would not be focusing on her. She had told her mother this, and logically she had known it, but emotionally it had not hit her. The strange thing was it felt different, but not worse. There were positive sides to each experience. There were less people watching her, she had a less prestigious part, but she also felt strangely relaxed. There was less pressure. And she could enjoy watching the parts of the ballet that she was not in, where if she had been dancing Swanhilda she couldn't have. Kaitlyn suddenly shook her head. *Don't try and fool yourself, Kaitlyn. This sucks, and you really, really wish you could be out there dancing Swanhilda right now.* Kaitlyn watched Grace *port de bras* backwards with about half the depth that she could have done it with.

Alexandra waited in the wings as the music began to play

for the evening performance. "Da da, dadada, dadada, dada," she hummed to herself. Across the stage she could see the house that Mr. Yu had worked so hard on, painted in grey and brown. At the top of the house was an open window, and Keiko sat there, staring outside blankly. She was playing a life-size doll made by the eccentric toy-maker, Doctor Coppélius. The beautiful doll was named Coppelia, and she sat there reading a book.

It was time. Alexandra ran out, dancing a light and happy variation. She played Swanhilda, the doll's neighbour. Through her dance she tried to make friends with the doll, not realizing that Coppelia was not alive. At the end, realizing that Coppelia was still ignoring her, Alexandra's Swanhilda ran off, sulking. But not far; Alexandra ran into her house, across from Coppelia, where she had an excellent view of her fiancé, Frantz, trying to flirt with Coppelia. The doll was as unresponsive to him as she was to Swanhilda, and Frantz left. Swanhilda was left filled with jealousy and curiosity.

Alexandra loved this ballet. Frantz and Swanhilda were both irresponsible brats, the spoiled darlings of their village. It was a fun contrast to the tragedy and drama of *Giselle*, or *Swan Lake*, or *La Bayadère*, even. It was during Act II that it happened. Alexandra had watched Julian's Frantz be drugged by Delilah's Doctor Coppélius. Doctor Coppélius wanted to take the life force out of Frantz and put it inside his doll. Unfortunately, Swanhilda was currently dressed as Coppelia, and she was forced by the circumstances to come alive and dance like a puppet led by Doctor Coppélius. Alexandra was doing an *echappe*, when she felt her arch go over too far, and that was when she knew that something was wrong. It was during an awkward *pas de deux* of sorts that her foot gave out. She was supposed to be guided by Doctor Coppélius, and, while Delilah held her, the choreography dictated that she was to half-fall, held by Delilah, as if she was knocked off balance by Doctor Coppélius, or was simply refusing to dance with him. Alexandra fell, but she slipped, and when Delilah caught her, Alexandra's foot twisted at an angle that it simply couldn't handle. Alexandra's face went white under her foundation, but Delilah did not notice that anything was wrong. Delilah continued to play her part of the eccentric old man, walking off. Alexandra was supposed to walk like a doll to the corner and then begin a *diagonale* of *chaine* turns.

She walked over, but as she stood in the corner, she was not sure that she was going to be able to do it. She stretched out her right foot in front of her, preparing. *And one …*

Taylor was hanging out beside Mr. Yu, watching Alexandra dance and swinging her legs as she sat on one of the prop tables. She didn't have to dance for a bit. Mr. Yu stood beside her, intermittently barking out commands to the tech crew. Taylor was not supposed to be sitting on that table, but Mr. Yu was ignoring it for now. He suddenly stepped forward, staring at the stage. "Alexandra," he said. "Not okay."

"What?" Taylor said, even though he had been talking to himself.

Mr. Yu looked at her. "When Alexandra come off, you go on. Okay?"

Taylor nodded, her stomach suddenly spinning.

"Mao!" Mr. Yu said, calling her over. "Take out hairpiece; be ready to help her change." Mao nodded, starting to quickly take the fake flowers out of Taylor's hair, trying not to wreck her bun.

Mr. Yu stood in the wings as Alexandra started to *chaine* toward them. She was supposed to stop and then go back to dancing with Doctor Coppélius, a dance that was supposed to trick him into thinking that he had lost control over his lovely Coppelia doll. Instead, Mr. Yu motioned for Alexandra to keep *chaine*-ing until she was offstage. She didn't look surprised, and the second she was hidden behind the wings she limped off and sat on the floor, taking off her shoe. She wasn't the important one right now, though. On stage, a startled Delilah had broken into an improvised comedy routine, acting surprised and shocked about the loss of her doll. Delilah was waving her beard and hands about for all she was worth, but it would only buy them a few seconds. Mr. Yu helped Mao pin Alexandra's headpiece in her hair and do up the hooks on her new costume, and then Taylor ran back on stage. "*Ganbate!*" Mao called in a whisper after her. On the floor, Alexandra had started to cry. Her foot was red and swollen, and the combination of the pain and disappointment over having to leave the stage was more than she could handle.

Julian had been onstage this whole time, but he was supposed to be drugged, passed out on Doctor Coppélius's thick wooden kitchen table. In the interests of curiosity (and not forgetting to wake up!) he had kept his eyes open. Still, it was disorienting to be only able to look in one direction, and have one Swanhilda *chaine* past you, and then a few seconds later have different one pass by. *Taylor? What the?* He watched her dance a solo as Doctor Coppélius watched, marvelling at his creation. She finished, and now it was time for Frantz to slowly wake up. Taylor began to hurry around Doctor Coppélius's house, ripping up his spell book, starting up his other mechanical dolls, and generally being a nuisance. Julian firmly pushed down all thoughts of what could have happened to Alexandra, and focused on what he was going to dance next. He needed to; his memory of the steps was shaky at best.

As they took a bow, Julian felt like flying. He looked down at Taylor; her expression reflected how he felt. They had done it! They had danced their very first principal roles, and they'd been okay. Maybe not brilliant; maybe they had made some mistakes, and perhaps Julian might've slightly re-choreographed bits that he had forgotten; but it was over and they had done it. To Julian, it felt like the first time he had jumped off the high diving board at the public pool. He'd done it once, and nothing bad had happened, so he had decided that next time he would do a flip. The audience was cheering with awesome volume. *I guess they've heard about our Unfortunate Events,* Julian thought, as he grinned and bowed for the third time. *Not every school has to use both their understudies for the same show, or, not even an understudy at all.* The curtain began to close, and as it did they all began to scream, jumping up and down and hugging each other.

A few minutes later the curtain opened again, and Mr. Demidovski was standing in front of the microphone. To his right stood a lineup of the academy's teachers and staff: Mrs. Demidovski, dressed in black dress pants and a red shirt; Mr. Moretti, looking sullen; Mrs. Mallard, who had her "Queen of England" smile on and was beaming at everyone; Mrs. Castillo, who looked little and was clutching a bouquet of flowers with a serious expression on her face. Leah towered over everyone and was wearing a sparkly low-cut black tank top that didn't quite fit. Gabriel was there, wearing the same suit he wore to work every day, and Sequoia stood next to him in a sack-shaped baby-blue dress that made her look more washed-out than usual. Only Mr. Yu was missing.

"Where is Mr. Yu?" Mr. Demidovski demanded. Mr. Yu leapt out of the wings and took a place between Mrs. Mallard and Mrs. Castillo. He put his arms around their shoulders, grinning. They looked remarkably resigned to it for two dignified old ladies.

Mr. Demidovski began to talk, of the accomplishments of the school, of the awards won during the year, of how grateful he was for parental involvement ... Julian tuned out, bored. Finally Mr. Demidovski started to get to the interesting stuff. "Mr. Moretti will be leaving us," he said. "We are very glad he is going, sorry, excuse, we are sad that he is going, but glad that he is going to ..." Mr. Demidovski trailed off, as he realized too late that he had no idea what Mr. Moretti was going off to do. "We wish him the very best in his future endeavours. And, we would like to give out some scholarships. The students, the students working very hard this year, we want to reward, also reward the parents who give so much of money, of sweat." Mr. Demidovski nodded to Gabriel, who began to call out some names for small bursaries.

"Taylor ... Julian ... Chloe ... Kaitlyn ..." Mr. Demidovski read out the names from the stack of envelopes in his hands while handing them out. "Michael ... Tristan ..." After the first round of bursaries was distributed, Mr. Demidovski stepped back to the microphone. "We have also decided to start awarding new scholarship. Mrs. Castillo, please here."

Mrs. Castillo stepped up to the mike. "This scholarship, it is in memory of my daughter," she said.

"Speak up, Mrs. Castillo," Mr. Demidovski demanded.

"My daughter, Aurora Castillo, she loved dance very much ever since she was a little girl. She was very beautiful, very slim, very sweet. Is Alexandra here?" Mrs. Castillo looked around.

"Alexandra?" Mr. Demidovski echoed, taking the mike away from Mrs. Castillo. Gabriel whispered in Mr. Demidovski's ear. "Ah. She had to go to hospital — they think foot might be broken. Can anyone take and give to Alexandra?"

There was a moment's pause, and then Julian realized that no one was jumping to volunteer. "I'll do it," he offered. He walked up and took the envelope.

Mrs. Castillo reached up and hugged him, as if it had been him who was getting the scholarship, not Alexandra. Her wiry strong hands made Julian bend over so that she could whisper in his ear. "Tell Alexandra," Mrs. Castillo said through the sound of clapping, "that she was very good. Tell her that she was very beautiful, and I am very glad."

Julian nodded. "Okay."

"Good boy."

Taylor got changed quickly and met her mom, her dad, Vivienne, and Alison in the lobby. "Taylor, sweetheart, you looked like a princess out there!" Charlize exclaimed, hugging her. "I couldn't believe it when I saw you came on — I'm so glad —" Charlize quickly covered her mouth, realizing what she had been about to say in the very crowded theatre lobby. "It's very sad what happened to Lexi. But you were so good! Why was Julian dancing? I didn't know he was the understudy."

"It's a really long story, Mom," Taylor said, laughing. She turned to her dad.

"You were really good, princess," he said, smiling. "You looked just like a doll. Good thing you don't look like this one here, huh?" he laughed, pinching Alison's cheek affectionately. Alison brushed his hand away, scowling.

Taylor frowned at her dad's comment to Alison before asking slowly, "You liked it?"

"Yes! Well, I think you should have been cast before that other girl, if you ask me. You are twice as pretty as she is."

"Daddy. It's not about who looks best, it's about who's the best dancer."

"I know that," Steven said impatiently. They were walking out of the theatre, and he pushed open the door, leading them outside. "How about we go get something to eat, huh? And Taylor, have you thought any more about moving out to L.A., trying to focus on acting? We could try to get you some modelling work, too, Vivienne has *great* contacts." He hugged his Vivienne, who appeared to be mute.

"Yes. No," Taylor said firmly. "Yes, I have thought about it, no, I don't want to. Thanks, though."

Steven frowned. "Why not?"

Taylor shrugged. "I don't know."

"What do you mean you don't know?" Steven persisted. "That doesn't make sense, it isn't logical. Come on, you must have an answer."

"Well," Taylor said slowly, "I can always do acting later. Dancing I have to work on now. Also, I can always act while I'm dancing, like I did tonight, but I couldn't dance while I act."

"That is true," Steven was forced to concede. "They would think it very strange on set if you started to jump during a scene. You might have a point, princess. But remember, the offer is always open. And Vivienne makes great pancakes, if that sways your choice any."

"I'm good. Mom makes good pancakes, too."

Julian rubbed the makeup off his face, using liberal amounts of makeup remover. *That's better.* It was all right for the girls, they were used to wearing makeup. The mascara made his eyes water. "Julian!"

Julian turned around, unable to see whoever was speaking. The water had washed the makeup remover *into* his eyes, and that stuff *stung*. "Just a second, I'm dying, slash going blind." Julian felt his way to the roll of paper towel beside the sink and dried his eyes." He turned around.

"Oh, hi, Theresa!" He noticed that he still had eyeliner left in the creases of his eyes, and he quickly tried to rub it off, as it made him look a bit frightening.

"Congratulations!"

"Thanks." Julian stood there awkwardly. He had been right and Tristan had been wrong; it did feel creepy having read her biography to the end.

Theresa sat down in the chair next to him, completely uncaring that it was the boys' change room. "Have you decided what you are going to do for summer school yet?"

Julian shook his head. "I have no idea."

"It will all work out. If nothing else, you can always stay at the academy for summer school."

"Yeah, hopefully." *If I can pay the homestay fees …*

Theresa looked at him. "Is something wrong, Jules?"

Julian shrugged. "No, I'm fine," he said. "Just … it feels a bit weird to be done for the year, you know?"

"Yes," Theresa said, laughing. "Well, I'll leave you to get ready, then, you must be exhausted." She hugged him and kissed his forehead. "You are going to be very good, Julian. You showed everyone that tonight."

Kaitlyn walked out to meet her mom and dad. Jeff looked very confused. "Kaitlyn," he said, "why didn't you tell me that you weren't the lead this time?"

Kaitlyn stared at him. "I thought Mom told you."

"I thought that you told him," Cecelia said, shocked.

Jeff looked upset. "It feels really good to be in the loop," he complained. "Last I heard, you got the lead and everybody was happy? What happened? When did things change?"

"Around January," Kaitlyn said flatly. "That's when I found out that I wasn't going to be dancing Swanhilda. Then I found out that I definitely wasn't going to be a week ago."

"Why didn't you tell me?"

"Why didn't you ask?" Kaitlyn spotted Tristan and Nat leaving the theatre. "Just a second." She went running after them. "Hey," she said breathlessly.

"What's up?" Tristan asked pleasantly. This was an improvement over the cutting tone he would have used if Nat wasn't there, and Kaitlyn intended to take advantage of this new charitable side to him.

"So, are you going to come to the Academy next year?" Kaitlyn asked Nat.

"I don't know yet. There is an entire summer to get through. Why the interest, child?"

Kaitlyn shrugged. "Just curious."

"Curiosity killed the cat and made Alice take drugs. I advise you to avoid curiosity at all costs," Nat answered her. They turned to walk out of the theatre, leaving Kaitlyn behind them.

"In fact," Tristan added, stopping and half-turning around; "*I* don't even know if I am coming back to the academy in September." The theatre door closed behind him.

"What?" Kaitlyn protested.

Chapter Thirteen

The Fan Page of Vancouver International Ballet Academy
Have a good summer everyone! Remember to register
for summer school. Love, VIBA

Julian was standing downtown on Granville Street,
somewhere between Waterfront Station and Vancouver
City Centre Station. He looked at the piece of paper he
had in his hand with the list of buses he had to take to
get to Alexandra's.

"Hey!"

Is that a 5 or an 8?

"Julian!" Julian looked up. Leah had stopped illegally
in the middle of the street. He ran across and got in the
passenger seat, and Leah started the car again to the
sound of angry car horns.

"What's up?"

"I thought you'd be on the Island already."

"Going home tomorrow. I slept for too long today
to finish stuff and still make the last ferry back," Julian
said sheepishly.

"Where you headed, then?"

"I said I'd give Alexandra her scholarship — she
hurt her foot really bad last night, in the middle of
the show."

"I know. I was in the audience. You know what, I'll drive you. I wanted to see how she was doing, anyway."

"It's okay, you don't have to do that — I can bus." Julian held out his paper filled with directions as evidence of his bussing abilities.

"I don't have to do anything, Julian," Leah said dryly. "I could move to the Congo if I wanted to. I want to talk to you."

"Oh. Cool. Sweet. Um, what about?"

"How would you like a job?" Leah said bluntly. "I need somebody to teach my recreational ballet classes, and maybe sub for me on the junior competitive ballet classes."

Julian stared at her.

"You're going to have to prove that you can talk," Leah added.

"Yes, of course!" Julian said. His voice cracked, apparently choosing that moment to hit puberty. "But, don't you teach those classes?"

"Yes, but I hate it," Leah admitted. "I don't like ballet anymore, Julian. I respect it; I don't enjoy it. I'd rather be putting more energy into my contemporary classes and my competition pieces. You're a bit young, but you have the prestige of going to the academy and training with Theresa Bachman, you're good with kids, and you love ballet."

Julian gulped. "Like, when do you want me to start?"

Leah considered. "Well, we have summer school in early August, but I'm getting guest instructors in to teach that. We do have drop-in classes throughout the summer if you are comfortable teaching ten-to-twelve-year-olds. You'll be fine, just make sure they don't all get crushes on you. Be mean."

Julian considered. "And then I could work with Frida and we could actually create some repertoire!" he said, excited.

"Yes," Leah agreed.

"Wait." Julian stopped, his face falling. "I don't know if I can afford to pay the homestay fees all summer on that though. I don't want to be rude, but how much do you think I'd be making?"

"If it doesn't pay Mr. Yu's rent, I'll get you set up somewhere else. Your parents will contribute something, right? I mean, you're sixteen. If you want to, then we have a deal," Leah said firmly.

"So down!" Julian agreed. He let out a whistle, barely able to sit in his seat. "I need to go plan stuff out. I need to talk to George! He'll know which ballet-class CDs are the best."

Alexandra was sitting in her room, watching TV. She looked up as Julian walked in. "Oh, hey. What's up, Julian? Congrats on doing so well last night."

"Thanks," Julian said, smiling. He looked at her, confused; she looked different. *Oh. She's not wearing makeup. I don't think I've ever seen her not wearing makeup — that makes sense though, why would she put it on when she can't go anywhere?* "That's quite the moon boot you've got on there."

"Yeah," Alexandra agreed. "I was hoping for one of those cast things that people could sign, but —"

"This is much more fashionable," Julian assured her. "Astronauts are totally in this season."

Alexandra laughed. "I'd almost believe you if it weren't for the fact that you have, like, two pairs of jeans and four shirts and none of them are remotely in style."

"Hey," Julian said defensively. "They're my kind of style. This look can't be copied, you know, you're either born with it, or — you turn out like Lady Gaga."

"Cool about Tristan and Nat, hey?"

"Yeah."

"Of course, now Tristan's totally obsessed with getting into RBS … it'll probably make him work a lot this summer."

"Yeah. Leah offered me a job, so I'm probably going to be here in the summer, if everything works out."

Alexandra looked at her moon boot. "Me too, apparently."

"How long is that thing going to be on for?"

Alexandra's lip quivered. "Oh, um …six months, about."

"Wow. That is so crappy."

"Yup."

"Oh, I found out about Isaac," Julian said, breaking down into giggles.

"Oh, I forgot you were still reading Theresa's biography! What did happen to Isaac? I can't remember."

"He decided to quit ballet and open a restaurant business, and then that failed, so then he went to teach snowboarding at Whistler and now he owns a small hotel up there. Apparently Theresa was really upset because he was her favourite partner ever, and she thought that he was wasting his life." Julian started to giggle again. "Oh, and the artistic director freaked out and gave an interview basically ripping him apart for quitting, probably because Theresa was, like, depressed and stuff for almost a year after he quit."

"That doesn't sound like anything you would do," Alexandra said sarcastically. "Not remotely."

"So, how's the truth-or-dare stuff going?" Julian asked suddenly.

"Uh —" Alexandra stared at him, embarrassed and confused. "What do you mean?"

"Well, since you aren't going to be dancing for six months, you probably don't have to do that anymore, right?"

"It doesn't work that way, Julian."

"How do you know?" Julian said reasonably. "I think you should try."

"What about you? Are you going to be not smoking all summer?"

"That's different."

"No, it's not. Julian, I think you should stop. If you are really going to be a good ballet dancer, which everybody seems to think you can be, you need to quit."

"So do you," Julian said firmly. "Smoking can't kill me. Your problem can."

They both suddenly had the same idea. "Let's try to both quit, and see who lasts the longest," Julian said first.

"I think we should have some special circumstances clauses, though," Alexandra said warily.

"Okay. Um … I won't smoke weed unless someone gives it to me. If I pay for it, I lose. This way I'll save my money, too."

"And I won't throw up unless someone makes me eat. If I eat by myself and then throw it up, I lose."

"Deal."

"Julian!" Leah called up the stairs. "If we go now I can drive you to the ferry. You'll make it in a car."

Julian jumped off Alexandra's bed. "Ow, careful," Alexandra protested.

"Sorry."

"So, I guess I'll see you around this summer? And by that I mean you'd *better* visit me because I'll be bored out of my head."

"Sure," Julian said, grinning.

Julian ran downstairs and got in Leah's car. He stared dreamily out the window at the sky. *It's summer.* It was going to be a good summer. It suddenly occurred to him that he knew exactly what he would like to get for a tattoo, if he got a tattoo, it would be a platypus. It seemed to sum up exactly how he felt about his life. Part of everything, and different at the same time. Perhaps he would think on it for a bit, though. Did he really want to be the dude with the platypus tattoo?

TAKE A SNEAK PEEK AT THE FOURTH BALLET SCHOOL CONFIDENTIAL BOOK, *DÉJÀ VU MUCH?*

Taylor Audley
I cant beleive that summer is over and Nutcracker rehearsal starts in a week! Gonna miss all teh good freinds I made :(:(

The air in Vancouver was crisp and the sweet smell of rotting leaves filled the city streets, but the sun still shone brightly. Taylor was very busy unpacking her suitcase. She had spent the summer studying dance at a summer intensive in California, and then another intensive in Seattle, and finally she had visited her father in L.A. and done all of her back-to-school shopping. It had been a great summer — all she had to do to remember that was look at the five-hundred-plus photos she had taken — but it was good to be back in Vancouver, and in her own room. "I even missed the rain," she said out loud. She'd been talking to Julian while she was away, and according to him it had rained in Vancouver for most of the summer. The skies were clear and blue now though; everyone thought they were going to have an Indian summer.

"What?"

Taylor turned around and saw her little sister, Alison, standing in the doorway. "Hey, Ali! Nothing. Just talking to myself." She began to pull out the results of her shopping. Her father was much more fun to go shopping with than her mother. Her father just stood around and sent emails on his BlackBerry while she shopped, but her mother would have actual opinions, and her opinions were always lame. Taylor pulled out a sweet new jacket. It was warm brown leather, and looked amazing with her blond hair. She put it to the side next to a pale pink tank top, a new pair of jeans, and a new yellow push-up bra.

Alison walked in and rubbed the leather between her fingers. "It's so soft — can I try it on?"

"Sure." Taylor shrugged, pulling the rest of her stuff out of the suitcase. *There!* She pulled out her most important purchase: a box of leotards. She had five new leotards, and she was pretty sure that none of them were sold in Canada. Also a new bottle of Jet Glue — it hardened her shoes and also wasn't available in Canada — and several new pairs of tights. She put almost everything away in her drawer and kept out one bodysuit, a purple halter top, and a new pair of tights to wear the next day.

The doorbell rang. "Were we expecting anyone?" Taylor heard her mother call as she went to answer it. Alison went running out of the room to see who it was, still wearing Taylor's new jacket.

"Not me," Taylor shouted back to her mother. She dumped the rest of her bag on the ground and lay down on the bed. She had done enough unpacking for today. It was so weird having a room to herself; she was going to miss having the company of other dancers, but it was nice to have some privacy finally. Even while she had been in Seattle with her dad she hadn't had privacy, because her dad's girlfriend, Vivienne, would not stop "dropping by" and "peeking in" on her. Vivienne was determined to be friends with her, which Taylor wouldn't mind if she found Vivienne at all likable, but she found her condescending and fake. Also, she thought that she wore far too much black and red.

"Taylor!"

"Coming ..." *I wonder who it is?*

Charlize was sitting on the couch, her hands awkwardly clutching her kneecaps, and Alison was sitting on the stairs eavesdropping. On the other side of the couch was a boy that Taylor didn't recognize at first. "Oh!" she exclaimed as he turned around. "Nat, what are you doing here?"

"Taylor, we need to talk," Charlize said quickly. "Nat, do you want some pop? Juice?"

Nat shook his head. "I'm good," he said, his voice clipped. He had his own unique accent, half fake upper-class British, half something unrecognizable that caused him to roll certain words. "You go ahead, I need to call my mother, anyway. She told me to phone her when I got off the plane, and that was three hours ago — she's probably called the embassy already." He pulled out his phone, and Charlize ushered Taylor out of the living room and into the kitchen.

"What is he doing here?" Taylor demanded.

"Well, I was going to tell you," Charlize said apologetically. "Things have been a little tight around here, financially, with your father getting ready to marry

Vivienne and everything — anyway, I volunteered to take in a homestay student, and I asked for a girl. Gabriel told me that Lux was coming tomorrow night, but Nat just showed up, and I don't know what to do!"

"Call Gabriel," Taylor said reasonably.

"You are so smart sometimes," Charlize said, relief flooding her face. "Okay, that's what I'll do. I'll do it right now." She took out her phone and called the academy, her left hand on her hip as she prepared to argue. Taylor opened the fridge door and took out the chocolate milk, pouring herself a glass.

"Gabriel? Yes, it's Charlize — yes ... Well, yes, that's what I am calling about. You see, Nat showed up ... Lux's older brother ... excuse me? ... Well, that's not what you said in August ... no, I would really prefer not to ... "

Taylor snuck a peek out at the living room. Nat was on the phone, speaking quietly and intently. *He is* so *not calling his mother*, she thought, slightly amused.

"Well, no, of course he needs a place to stay, but this is not what we agreed on ... I see ... well, yes, but, yes, I realize ... he can stay for a week, but I want to talk to you when the school opens tomorrow.... All right, I will see you then." Charlize hung up, and turned to Taylor. "Now what?" she asked rhetorically. "I guess Nat will be staying with us for a week until I figure out what happened with the original arrangements. I hope he likes pink, because I was going to put Lux in the spare room, and I completely redid it with all of your old stuff."

"Oh wow." Taylor started to giggle. She could not wait to see Nat's face when he saw his room.

They walked out into the living room. "Okay then, bye. Love you. Ciao." Nat quickly hung up his phone.

"Was your mother all right?" Charlize asked.

"Oh, yeah, she was fine," Nat assured her. "Just freaking out as usual — you know how mothers are. She would prefer it if I was locked in a padded chamber with my favourite teddy bear."

Charlize laughed, for a little too long and a little too loudly. "Do you want to see your room? I'm afraid I decorated it for a girl …"

"I am sure that it's fine," Nat reassured her. He and Taylor followed Charlize downstairs to the spare room.

Taylor was watching Nat's face when he got his first look at his new home, and she was impressed to see that he managed to keep his face neutral. She used to be really into Hannah Montana and butterflies when she was younger, and there were more shades of pink and purple used in her room than in the average Barbie dollhouse. She noticed that Charlize had taken down her old Backstreet Boys and Justin Timberlake posters and replaced them with Taylor Lautner and One Direction. "Mom," she protested. "Even if this room was for Lux, she's fourteen, not twelve."

"You still liked this stuff when you were fourteen," Charlize protested.

"Yeah, but I knew it wasn't cool," Taylor defended herself. "That's why I took it down."

"It's all good," Nat assured them. "The bed looks comfortable, and to be honest, that's all I'm concerned with at the moment. I'll just bring my stuff in, and then if you don't mind, I'd like to pass out for long time."

"Oh, of course," Charlize said quickly. "We'll help you with the suitcases …" They helped him drag the suitcases into the room and Alison watched surreptitiously from the staircase.

When they were done Nat yawned ostentatiously. "We'd better let you sleep," Charlize said. "Do you want anything to eat?"

"No, I'm fine," Nat assured her, smiling. "Good night." He closed the door firmly behind him when they exited, and Taylor thought she could hear the click of the lock.

"I don't like this," Charlize murmured as they climbed the stairs. "It's one thing to take in a fourteen-year-old girl, another to take in a sixteen-year-old boy."

"Whatever," Taylor said. "I think it's going to be fun."

"Fun!" Charlize walked off to the kitchen, and Taylor went back to her bedroom. She still had a lot of unpacking to do, but instead she took out her laptop and went on Facebook. She had a message waiting for her from Zack. Zack went to her high school, and they had been talking a lot this summer. They had even managed to meet up for a day in L.A., because he'd had a screen test. He hadn't ended up getting the role, but he'd made it pretty far, and it had been nice to see him.

Hey.

How was the flight? I was going to make fun of "yor" spelling in your last message, but then I realized you were probably exhausted from shopping and I decided to give you a break. Aren't I nice? Anyway, do you have any free time tomorrow? I know you're too cool for school what with dance and everything, but maybe we could meet up after you're done dance. I want to see your stupid face again so I remember how much hotter I am. <3

Taylor looked at the message for a while, wondering how to reply. She had dance from 9:30 a.m. to 4:30 p.m. tomorrow, but she could see him after — the problem was, she didn't know whether she wanted to. When she first met Zack they'd had a lot in common, but he was actually really smart, and sometimes he made her feel bad about school and stuff without meaning to. He would just use really long words and stuff, or talk about people that he assumed that she would know, and then when she didn't know what he was talking about she would feel dumb. Like the spelling thing. *What person our age cares about spelling, anyway?* She deliberated for a while, and then realized that she knew the perfect person to ask for advice. If she was brave enough.

Taylor walked lightly out of her room, carrying her laptop. She made it past the kitchen and down the stairs without her mother hearing her. From the sounds of it her mother was making dinner. Downstairs she listened at Nat's door; it was very quiet inside. "Nat," she whispered. "Nat!" She knocked lightly. She heard sounds of movement, and a drawer being opened and closed, and then finally Nat opened the door.

"What?" he asked. He didn't sound happy, and his usually neat hair was tousled and clumped on one side.

"Sorry," Taylor said. "I just really need your advice. Are you like busy or sleeping or something?"

Nat sighed. "Well, now I'm not. Come in."

Taylor came in and sat at the edge of Nat's pink bed, setting the laptop down. "I need help," she admitted.

"With what?"

"Read this."

Nat sat down beside her and read the entire message in a few seconds. "He critiqued your spelling? Smooth. What's your issue, babycakes?"

"I don't know what to do," Taylor explained. "I'm not sure if I like him, and I don't know how to tell him that, or if I should tell him that, because what if I do like him?"

Nat sighed. "Don't you have any friends to ask?" he said. "All right then. I'm going to help you, because I am just that nice. Pass me that pen and notebook from the dresser."

Taylor passed them to him, confused.

Nat lay down on the bed and began drawing a chart. On the top there were two sections: *Pro*, said one, and the other read *Con*. "All right. Now why would you want to date Zack?"

Taylor thought. "He's nice."

"Nice. *Bam*. Poor kid."

"He's kind of cute. Like, he's sort of small, but he's cute."

"Cute, pro. And, con, midget."

"And, if I dated him I'd probably be like the first person at the academy to have a boyfriend."

"Really?"

"Well, obviously Tristan is dating you, but like of the girls."

"Okay. Pro, competitive instinct."

"And he knows about a lot of parties."

"The kid has connections ..."

"But my mom would probably not let me go to most of them, plus I have rehearsal all the time."

"No time." Nat finished the list. "It looks like there are a lot more pros than cons. So why the hesitation?"

Taylor shrugged. "I don't know," she said honestly. "I just think I like him more as a friend than a boyfriend, and I know he doesn't see me that way."

"Well —" Nat considered "— I would meet up with him tomorrow and see how it goes. You'll be more likely to know what you want to do when you are face to face with him."

"Okay," Taylor agreed quickly, glad to have someone else make her decision for her. "Thanks."

"Taylor!"

Taylor winced, hearing her mother calling. "Coming, Mom!" She stood up. "What's that?" She picked up an orange bottle of pills from the counter. "Adderall? You have ADHD, too? That's so cool, I didn't know that."

"Hmm," said Nat. "Don't take this the wrong way, you're charming, but I really want to go back to sleep, okay?" He passed Taylor her laptop, and she left.

"What were you doing down there bothering Nat?" Charlize asked, sounding annoyed. She was attempting to clean up some spilled tomato sauce.

"Nothing! Geez, I just wanted to see if he had towels."

"He has towels, Taylor. Go get your sister for dinner."

"Alison!" Taylor shouted.

Charlize winced. "I said 'go get your sister.' What part of that did you not understand?"

Alison walked in to the kitchen on her hands, falling in a heap just before she reached the table.

"What are you doing?" Taylor asked, curious.

"I decided that I want to work for the Cirque de Soleil when I grow up," Alison said calmly. "Is that boy not going to eat any dinner?"

"Nope," Charlize said. "He's trying to get some sleep, not that he can do that with your sister constantly interrupting him."

"Hey!" Taylor protested. "It was only once."

Charlize spooned out some pasta on both of their plates. "I can't believe that summer is over already," she said, sighing. "I haven't even seen you all summer, Taylor, and now school is starting. We need to make some time to do family stuff."

"Mom, we see each other all the time." Taylor reached for the parmesan jar and began sprinkling it liberally.

"Oh!" Charlize said, suddenly, snapping her fingers. "That reminds me — your father phoned me. Apparently *Vivienne* thinks you should see a nutritionist."

"Who cares what *Vivienne* thinks?"

"Why do you guys hate Vivienne?" Alison asked.

"We don't hate Vivienne, Alison," Charlize said at the same time that Taylor said, "Because she's Vivienne."

"Anyway, in this case, she might be right," Charlize admitted. "You eat straight carbs, Taylor. You have to start getting some protein and vegetables into your diet."

Taylor jabbed her pasta with her fork. "I feel fine," she argued.

"Tell me about California," Charlize asked, changing the subject. "How was the end of show performance?"

"I already told you about it," Taylor said. "Oh, but I forgot to tell you — I saw Anna there!"

"What? Really?"

"Yeah! It was cool to see her."

"Does she miss the academy at all?"

"No. She hasn't gotten any better, though. She's still at about the same level as she was when she left. I almost have higher extensions than her now."

"Was she in your level?"

"No, the level above."

"Oh."

Crash.

They stayed sitting for one second, and then as one they all ran downstairs in the direction of the noise. Charlize knocked on Nat's door. "Is everything all right in there?" she asked solicitously. She pushed open the door without waiting for an answer.

Nat stood in the middle of the room, looking confused. The wooden dresser that had been sitting on the back wall was now lying on its side. "I'm not entirely sure how that happened," he said, sounding bewildered. "I dropped something behind the back of the dresser, and the next thing I knew the bloody thing was on the ground. Pardon the language."

"Oh, that's all right," said Charlize in a tone that clearly meant that it was *not* all right. "Here. You take an end." Together Charlize and Nat managed to set the dresser right side up again. "All right then. Good night,"

Charlize said firmly. "You, too, Alison and Taylor. It's the first day of school tomorrow and I don't want to hear any whining about how tired you are tomorrow."

Taylor obediently went to bed, but once she had gotten changed into her pajamas, brushed her teeth, laid out her clothes for the next morning, checked Facebook, texted *kk :)* to Zack, and climbed under the covers, she still wasn't tired. She was excited to go back to the academy, but it felt weird being back. The summer had been so fun and different, and she had met so many people, both other dancers and teachers. She'd made new friends with people from all over the world, and her new teachers had seemed to think that she was really good. Even Anna had been kind of nice to her in California; they had eaten dinner together in the cafeteria a few times. It was going to be strange to be back at the academy.

Taylor rolled over and pressed her eyes shut in an attempt to go to sleep, but she still couldn't. It was too warm. She got out of bed and opened her window, letting the fresh night air blow in. As she stood by the window, she smelled something strange. Something smoky.

She walked lightly out into the hall, trying to figure out where the smoke was coming. *Oh.* It was downstairs. She was about to go and wake up her mother to tell her that something was on fire, when she remembered that that Nat's room was downstairs. She decided to sneak down instead.

Nat's room was firmly closed, which Taylor was beginning to suspect was normal for him. She knocked twice, quietly. He didn't come to the door, so she walked out into the garden and around to where Nat's window was. The window was open, and Nat's head was half out, as he smoked a cigarette. He blinked once, but other than that his face did not register much surprise. "Hello."

"Hello." Taylor stood awkwardly. The grass was a bit wet from the sprinkler, and her feet were cold. "I smelled the smoke, so I thought something was burning."

"Well, it's not," Nat reassured her.

Taylor wasn't sure what to say next.

"Do you want to come in and talk?" Nat asked finally. "I'm a bit bored. The sleeping idea isn't working out for me so far."

"Okay." Taylor walked back around, and this time Nat opened the door to let her in. She noticed that he shut it tightly after her.

Taylor sat on his bed. "How come you're coming to the academy?" she asked. "Everyone thought that you were going to the Royal Ballet School."

Nat went back to the window, sitting on the sill so he could tap his ash out onto Charlize's flower bed. "Well," he said slowly. "My parents didn't really like the idea of me going to England. They're thinking of relocating to Canada in a few years, and I have family in Toronto."

"But, that's not a good reason," Taylor protested. "You should have talked to them."

"I also didn't get in," Nat admitted quietly.

"What?"

He shrugged. "I got in to the summer school, and I thought they'd offer me a position for the fall, but they didn't. It was rather upsetting at the time, but now

I guess it's all right. I mean, Theresa Bachman teaches here, right?"

"Not really," Taylor corrected. "She was giving me and Julian privates, but that's pretty much it."

"Oh. Lovely." Nat finished his cigarette and laid it on the sill. "That was pretty much the only thing I was looking forward to."

"Hey!" Taylor protested. "The academy is a good school!"

"It has managed to train good dancers," Nat corrected. "There's a difference. I don't know. I suppose I am feeling pressed. Grade twelve and all that. Got to get a job by the end of next year, or my parents are determined that I go to university."

"Oh. That sucks," Taylor said. She watched Nat light another cigarette. "Can I try?"

"No. Cigarettes are bad for you. I'm quitting, actually." Nat ran his hand through his hair, looking frustrated, "Let's talk about something a little less stressful than my life."

"My parents want me to be an actor," Taylor offered.

"What about university?"

"Oh, they don't think I'd be able to go. They want Alison to go. She's really smart."

"Well, being an actor wouldn't be so bad if it worked out."

"I know. But I don't want to be an actor, I want to be a ballet dancer."

Nat didn't answer, so Taylor searched for something to say. "You've lived in a lot of places, hey?" she said finally.

"Yeah," Nat agreed. "Our home has always been Hawaii, but I've lived in New York, Bristol, Tobago, Amsterdam, Honduras, Johannesburg, Frankfurt ... I think I'm leaving places out, but I'm too lazy to remember. I've never lived in a small town though — that would be the strangest thing for me. I want to try some day. I want neighbours who watch me every day and gossip about the lunatic things I do, and say hi to me in the grocery store. It'd be like being famous, except if you found you didn't like it, you could always just move away." Nat pointed at the shelf across the room. "What's that?"

"My old paint set," Taylor said. "I haven't used it in ages."

Nat put his cigarette out on the sill and walked over, picking up the dark wood box and setting it down on the floor. He sat down and opened it up. "Do you mind if I use it?" he asked.

"I don't care," Taylor assured him. "I'm hopeless with paint."

"Come here," Nat ordered, patting the seat beside him. "I'm going to show you our place in Tobago." He poured a bit of water from his water bottle into its lid, and opened up a tube of blue, squeezing a small amount onto a thick paintbrush. "The water there isn't like the water here," he explained. "Here, you look down and maybe you see seaweed, rocks, but mostly it's a darker blue, and you can't see very far or at all below the surface. In Tobago, you can see to the bottom." He wetted the paint brush constantly to get the acrylic light enough, mixing blues with greens.

Taylor sat with her arms around her knees as she watched him paint. "You're really good," she said. "It's cool that you can paint. I can't do really anything except dance, and some days I think that I'm not really even any good at dancing."

"You're good," Nat reassured her, concentrating on creating the texture of the waves crashing on the pale sand of his shoreline. "You did well in that contemporary *pas de deux* you did at YAGP."

"But what if I'm not good enough?" Taylor asked.

"Well," said Nat, "that's the question, isn't it? I guess we'll find out."

Taylor yawned. "Your house was pretty," she said, watching him sketch the outline.

"It was all right." Nat shrugged. "It was mostly the water I loved. Lux didn't like it in Tobago because she had nowhere good to train, so my parents left her in Hawaii with my aunt and uncle so she could keep going to school there. She's always been more driven than me."

"That sucks."

Nat considered. "That depends. On whether it works out or not. You see, if I don't get a job with a dance company, I have other things to explore. I have the ocean of Tobago, I have my collection of coats, I have my love of physics and Allen Ginsberg. If Lux doesn't find a job, which admittedly is very unlikely, she will be devastated."

"I guess even I have acting," Taylor said slowly. "I'm pretty sure my dad could find me work."

"And you have Zack," Nat pointed out. "Lux would never have time for a boy. She's too focused."

Taylor yawned again. "Go to sleep," Nat told her. "I'll wake you up when the painting's finished."

"Okay." Taylor lay down on her old bed and almost immediately fell asleep, lulled by the comforting smells of her old blankets, the smoke from Nat's cigarettes, the acrylic paint, and the fall air blowing through the open window. Just before she fell asleep, she thought of something. *Julian would love living in Tobago. He could pretend that he was a pirate. I wonder who is going to be the Nutcracker Prince this year.*

Also in the Ballet School Confidential series by Charis Marsh

Love You, Hate You (Book 1)
978-1554889617
$12.99

Kaitlyn, Taylor, Alexandra, and Julian are all students at the Vancouver International Ballet Academy where ballet and drama dominate everyone's lives.

Kaitlyn was the star at her old school, but the competition at VIBA is fierce and her reputation as a prodigy is threatened. About to turn fifteen years old, Taylor is a bit of a scatterbrain. She's got a lot of potential, but the teachers are frustrated with her lack of confidence, and her troubles at school aren't helping. Alexandra has done everything right, and she's determined to become a dancer, but the teachers at VIBA seem to be against helping her. Julian, at fifteen, loves dance, so going to a professional ballet school seems fun — even if it does take over every aspect of his life.

It's only their first semester, but these four students will have to push themselves to their limits to make it through their first major performance, *The Nutcracker*, and continue on the path to becoming professional dancers.

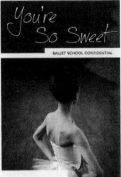

You're So Sweet (Book 2)
978-1459704176
$12.99

The Vancouver International Ballet Academy has opened its doors after the winter break, and everyone is back! Julian is finding it difficult to concentrate on dance because of his family; his teachers think he could be great if he could just focus. Kaitlyn believes she's the best dancer, but her body type is getting in the way of her (and her mother's) dance ambitions, tempting her to tell lies. Alexandra is as focused as usual, but others don't seem to understand how much time and energy she has to give to ballet if she wants to be the best. While Taylor is still criticized at VIBA, she's getting a lot of positive attention from outside — especially from a recently retired Canadian ballerina who's taken an interest in her and Julian. Who will get noticed in competition and the spring seminar? Whatever happens, someone's going to lose and someone's going to win.

www.dundurn.com